VISITING HOURS

Tagan Shepard

BELLA
BOOKS

2017

Bella Books, Inc.
P.O. Box 10543
Tallahassee, FL 32302

Printed in the United States of America on acid-free paper.

First Bella Books Edition 2017

Editor: Katherine V. Forrest
Cover Designer: Judith Fellows

ISBN: 978-1-59493-570-1

About the Author

Tagan Shepard has always spent quiet moments weaving stories in her head. It didn't occur to her until recently to take the time to write them down. Now that she's started, she can't seem to stop. When not writing, she makes her living in a hospital laboratory.

She is a cardio junkie, history buff, and unrepentant nerd, happily wasting countless hours of her life on video games and science fiction/fantasy of every stripe. She lives in Richmond, Virginia with her very patient wife and two rather surly cats.

Dedication

To my dearest wife.

Without love, there is no life, and so without you, there is no me.

Acknowledgments

Thank you to Deirdra McAfee for being the first person to call me a writer, long before I was even willing to call myself one. Also to Lavinia Moxey and Nathalie Oates for your invaluable insight. Bella Books and Jessica Hill took a chance on me and for that I will be eternally grateful. To Katherine V. Forrest for being the best editor a new writer could hope for. Archive of Our Own provided a venue for me to cut my teeth at this whole writing thing and gave me a forgiving and supportive audience. It is an invaluable resource and I am most grateful.

Writing is a solitary art and I have at times neglected the people in my life in favor of the people in my head. I'm lucky enough to have an incredibly supportive family who continue to love me despite my flaws. In particular, my wife Cris who looked at me one day and said, "Why don't you write a book?" Thank you from the bottom of my heart.

CHAPTER ONE

As the doors of Virginia Commonwealth University Medical Center slid open in front of Alison Reynolds, tension suffused her body. She'd never had a problem with hospitals until her best friend became a regular visitor to them. Now the smell of bleach and nitrile made her skin crawl and her heart ache. Worse yet, she had never been either a patient or a visitor here, and the lack of familiarity made her edgy. She had lived in Richmond most of her adult life, but never had a reason to come into VCU's hospital. It was the big one. The one where they took gunshots and major accidents. The one where people came to die.

Alison shook the thought from her head. It brought up too many ghosts. She needed to be in a positive frame of mind when she got to Beth's room. Her best friend had always been able to read her like a book. Whatever mood she arrived with today would immediately show. She needed to be happy. Or at least not scared.

She made for the information desk near the bank of elevators. At most hospitals, an elderly volunteer with a wide smile but little actual information to impart would occupy this space. Instead, she found a harassed-looking, middle-aged African-American woman finishing a phone call. Alison took up a position directly in front of her and waited, scanning the lobby and trying not to tap her nails on the stone countertop.

It was the middle of the day, and there were a fair number of people around. Alison caught her reflection in the tinted glass partition to her left and looked quickly away. She knew she didn't look her best today, but she wasn't keen on seeing the evidence. Her sleep had been fitful ever since Beth announced her most recent pregnancy. The bags under her eyes, only barely camouflaged by her simple makeup, were proof. Unfortunately, her best features were round brown eyes and high cheekbones, neither of which she could highlight in her present state. Now all she had to work with were thin lips, a long, arrow-straight nose, and a rounded jaw that at least kept her looking young. She wore her hair long and the thick, dark curls paired with the cheekbones drew a lot of comparisons to Julianna Margulies.

"Thank you for your patience, ma'am. How may I help you today?"

The woman at the information desk looked up at her with a warm smile. Almost as surprising as her kindness was her ability to give Alison detailed directions. More than one hospital in the area had left her frustrated and annoyed at the lack of knowledgeable staff. To find a person who could help her and do so pleasantly was a welcome surprise. She boarded an empty elevator, beginning to hope that this visit would go more smoothly than similar trips in the past.

Her hopes were dashed the minute the doors opened. The directions seemed relatively straightforward downstairs, but it didn't take long to get herself hopelessly lost. All the hallways looked the same. When she peeked into open doorways, the rooms all looked the same too. She had a room number, but the numbering system did not appear to follow any logical order. Then she turned a corner and the numbers suddenly had letters behind them. She tried to retrace her steps, but found herself in an open lobby she had never seen before.

A high counter ran around a central bank of desks and computers. She assumed that this was the unit nurses station, having seen similar setups before. Unfortunately, it was currently abandoned. The omnipresent beeps and tones announced themselves to a slew of empty chairs. Further along the hall stood a pair of elevators that bore no resemblance to the ones she rode up. People in lab coats milled around in front of them, but, as she started to make her way toward them, an elevator arrived and they all disappeared onto it without noticing her. She sighed in frustration and turned, looking again for someone to help her. Around the corner of the nurses station was a bench against the wall. Someone sat on the bench.

The woman there looked like she might be in her mid to late thirties, but the way she dressed and carried herself were at odds with that age. She was slouched forward over a cell phone, typing away with her elbows on her knees. Her blue jeans were worn and form-fitting, and the sleeves of a black V-neck T-shirt were bunched up around well-toned shoulders, several inches of colorful tattoos visible beneath the left sleeve. She had golden yellow hair cut short on the sides, pulled into gelled spikes on top. It wasn't quite a mohawk, but it belonged on one of Alison's students, not an adult. She guessed this woman was a graduate student or perhaps one of the more punky bike messengers popular on this end of town. Her thumbs flew across the screen of her smartphone with a strength and confidence that suggested she worked with her hands a lot. Alison judged that she pretended to be a sculptor or a drummer or something equally unemployable when she wasn't loitering in hospitals.

Alison turned away, trying to guess a direction based on the room numbers around her. She let out a long, frustrated breath.

"Can I help you find something?"

The voice was low and a little throaty, but with a cadence that exuded confidence. Alison turned. The woman stood, slipping the phone into the back pocket of her jeans with a motion that stretched the fabric of her T-shirt tight across her chest. Alison forced her gaze to the woman's face. She wore a gleaming smile, showing off impossibly white teeth and shockingly green eyes. Had it not been for her growing annoyance, Alison would have allowed herself a long moment to appreciate the woman in front of her. Today she really didn't have time.

"No. Thanks."

The obvious chill of her tone did nothing to dissuade the stranger, who took a step forward, her thumbs hooked in her back pockets. "Are you sure? You look sorta lost."

"I'm fine." Alison bit off the words as she pulled out the scrap of paper where she'd scribbled down Beth's room number. She looked at the hair spiking up a couple of inches over the woman's head and said, "I think I know where I'm headed."

She laughed and took a few steps forward, her hand outstretched. "If you let me see the room number, I can point you in the right direction. This place is a bit of a maze. Which unit are you looking for?"

Alison took a step back, her eyes flicking again to the woman's hair. "Thank you. But again, I don't need your help."

Her smile widened. "A blow-drier and a lot of texturizing cream."

"Excuse me?"

"It's how I get my hair like this. It's a lot of work, but I like it, so I put in the time. I assure you I don't yank out any brain cells when I style it."

"I'm sure you don't, and if I were looking for directions to a tattoo parlor or a head shop, you'd be the first person I'd ask. Now, if you'd excuse me?"

The woman laughed, crossing her arms over her chest, but not budging. "That would be a bad idea. I've never gotten a tattoo here in Richmond and I haven't smoked weed since undergrad. I can take a hint though. I was only trying to help, but I can see you're set on finding your own way. Best of luck."

She turned away just as a nearby door opened. A young man with a worried look on his face and a white lab coat in his hand hustled out of it.

"Doctor Baker! I'm so sorry! I think I got the stain out, but it's still a little damp."

She took the coat from him and slipped her arm through the sleeve. "Not a problem at all. I told you not to worry about it."

"Oh no! I couldn't let you walk around with a coffee stain on your coat. Especially when it was my clumsy fault it got there in the first place." He headed behind the half-wall that separated him from the nurses station. "Should I call Antepartum and let them know you're on your way?"

Her lab coat back on, the doctor started off down the hall Alison had come in from. "No need. Thanks!"

The young man turned to Alison and asked politely, "Can I help you, ma'am?"

Alison stared after the stranger's retreating form. Antepartum was Beth's unit and the annoying woman with the ridiculous hair said she was going there. And she was a doctor, no less. Alison turned back to the nurse. "I...No. Thank you. I know where to go."

She waited a beat to let the doctor get some distance. She followed quietly and slowly, but she had the sense the woman knew she was there. Alison couldn't take the thought of her smug smile when she caught Alison following. The very person from whom she'd refused help. Alison slowed to a crawl.

The slower pace gave her time to size up her quarry. Despite the coat's billowing tails, it was cut well, accentuating the doctor's broad shoulders and long legs, showing off a slim waist. The coat's long arms covered the tattoos, and the jeans didn't appear quite so unprofessional with square-toed black shoes. Most doctors wore business casual if they weren't in scrubs. On closer inspection, this outfit appeared only slightly more casual than that. Take away the hair and tattoos, and she had the physique of a woman who could talk Alison into almost anything on the third date. Shame it was wasted on such an immature individual.

She turned a quick corner and was suddenly out of sight. Alison cursed for allowing herself to become distracted and hurried to follow. She sped around the corner and nearly slammed into the other woman. She was leaning against the wall, arms crossed, wearing the smirk Alison dreaded.

"I *thought* I was being followed," she said good-naturedly.

Alison blushed. She smiled back, but she couldn't think of anything to say to defend herself.

The doctor laughed and stood straight, holding out her hand. "Jess Baker."

Alison took her hand and shook it. "Alison Reynolds."

"Pleased to meet you Alison Reynolds."

She tried not to notice the way her face heated up as the doctor's smile widened. "Likewise."

"Why don't I show you the way to Antepartum?"

The walk wasn't particularly long, but it was incredibly uncomfortable for Alison. She couldn't help mulling over the things she said and the looks she gave to this woman before discovering she was a doctor. Every memory made her cringe. She had not been polite. The quip about the head shop seemed particularly rude in hindsight. She longed for them to arrive at their destination so that she could leave the doctor behind, never to see her again.

Dr. Baker seemed perfectly at ease. Neither smug nor offended, she walked with her hands in her pockets and her eyes straight ahead. They turned into a wide hallway clearly marked with the unit name. How, Alison thought, could she have missed the foot-high, brushed nickel sign earlier? She could only guess it was from being preoccupied with worry.

A man leaning against the doorframe with his back to them blocked the way ahead. He was shouting into his cell phone.

"No. You're in the wrong place…I don't know! I'm in Antepartum…This is where Kimberly is…She hasn't had the baby…I know! Antepartum is for women who are just pregnant and Labor and Delivery is for women who are giving birth…I know it's confusing, Mom. It's like Latin or Greek or something, I don't know…Just stay there, I'll come get you and bring you here…Yeah, I'm headed there now…Look, it's not my fault! How was I supposed to know? They should make the names more clear! Okay. Okay. *Okay* Mom!"

He spun around, banging hard into Alison's shoulder as he passed without apologizing.

"I told you this place is a maze," Dr. Baker said with a shrug. "Everyone gets lost in here at least once."

Just ahead Alison finally saw the right room and decided it was time to make her graceful exit. She stopped, the doctor did as well. Turning with her most winning smile, she held out her hand.

"Well, thank you Doctor…Baker was it? Thank you for helping me navigate the maze. This is my stop."

"Please call me Jess." She smiled wide again, shaking Alison's hand. Motioning toward the door, she continued, "I'm afraid you can't get rid of me that easily. This is my stop too."

"You mean you're…"

"Ali? Is that you?"

It was Beth's voice, and Alison clung to it like a lifeline.

The room was bright and airy despite the oversized hospital bed and equipment crammed into the small space. Beth looked right at home on the bed, at least a half dozen pillows propped up behind her. Her growing belly was just visible under the blanket.

Alison had met Beth when they were both four years old. Their families were members of the same church, and Alison could remember with perfect clarity the day that a chubby little girl with a pair of puffy pigtails and skin the color of milky hot chocolate plopped down next to her on the carpet in Sunday school and asked her name. She had maybe three tiny teeth still in place and immediately showed them off in a wide grin. Alison smiled back shyly and they had been inseparable ever since.

When Alison's parents sent her to St. Catherine's, the all-girls private Catholic school in town, Beth had sweet-talked her parents into sending her as well. When she had gone to University of Richmond, Beth leveraged a basketball scholarship to follow. When Beth chose Boston College for law school, Alison went to Harvard for her master's degree and they picked an apartment halfway between campuses. Their only separation came when Alison studied in England, but Beth had made the transatlantic trip six times to visit even while studying for the bar and planning a wedding.

Alison all but sprinted to the bed and wrapped her friend in a hug. She tried not to let the worry lines show between her eyebrows when she drew back and perched on the edge of the mattress. She failed. Beth laughed, running her thumb over them to smooth them out.

Alison asked in a mock serious voice, "How's the Jell-O?"

Beth shook her head. "Lime."

"Blech! Inexcusable!"

"I know, right!" Beth looked over Alison's shoulder and asked, "Would it be so hard for you people to stock cherry?"

Dr. Baker stood near the door. "We save the cherry for the visiting heads of state and celebrities." She took a hesitant step in and continued, "If this is a bad time, I can come back."

"No, Doctor, please stay. Stephen was just here." Beth looked around the room as though she had misplaced her keys rather than her husband. "I'm sure he'll be right back."

"I've told you a thousand times to call me Jess."

A voice from the hallway said, "Then you only have a thousand more to go before it sinks in."

Stephen had to duck his head to enter the room. His blond hair was pulled back into a short ponytail that fell just to the collar of his shirt. As he stood to his full height of just over six and a half feet, he reached out to shake the doctor's hand. "Sorry to keep you waiting, Jess."

Stephen went straight to his wife's side and kissed her cheek. He smiled at Alison before retreating behind Beth and fluffing her pillows.

Dr. Baker pulled a rolling stool closer to the bed. "It's my fault. I had a run-in with a cup of coffee. Literally. Then I had to try and lose a tail." She smiled at Alison again and continued, "I'm afraid I couldn't shake her. She followed me here."

Alison knew the color was rising in her cheeks and forced herself to look nowhere in particular. Stephen saved her. "It's a good thing you brought her along. All of the decisions in this house go through Ali."

He laughed when he said it, but his nonchalance immediately chafed Alison's nerves. Stephen was a wonderful man and a doting husband, but she wished he would take life more seriously. He was a gifted landscaper and could be designing gardens for the governor if he had any ambition whatsoever. Instead, he made just enough money to contribute to the household expenses, and left work early every day to play with their two-year-old daughter.

"Well, then let's get to it!" Dr. Baker's entire aspect changed. Her eyes seemed to harden and a more neutral expression replaced the smile. "I've spoken to the Blood Bank. They're putting in an order for the transfusion. It will take a little bit of preparation, and the OR isn't available until tomorrow morning anyway. I was able to book it for ten o'clock."

The nonchalance evaporated from Stephen's voice. "How long will the transfusion take?"

"A couple of hours. Three at the most. After we're done, there will be some minor testing. Beth, you'll be under local anesthesia only. I'll need you to keep me updated on how you're feeling during and immediately after the procedure. You're going to take an active part, but don't worry, I'm going to talk you through everything."

"Can I be in the room?" Stephen asked.

"Not for this one, Steve. I'm sorry. There will be a lot of movement in and out of the room, so we need to limit the number of bodies. Just as a safety precaution. I was able to get the operating theater, though, so you can watch the whole thing from box seats."

Beth gripped Alison's hand like a vise, but her voice was steady as she addressed the doctor. "Tell me again what happens if you miss the vein?"

Jess rolled forward a few inches, her voice smooth as silk. "If we can't get to the umbilical vein for some reason, we can transfuse into his abdomen. He'll still get the blood, we just won't be able to give him as much. We might have to do a second procedure sooner than planned. Either way, he'll get what he needs."

All the organs in Alison's body had turned to cubes of ice. "I'm sorry to interrupt. I know I'm coming late to the party here, but exactly how late am I? What procedure? What blood?"

She looked at Beth and didn't even try to hide the worry. Her friend answered, "I'm sorry, Ali. It was just too much to tell you over the phone."

There was a light tap at the door and a stocky woman rolling a cart full of supplies stepped in. "Good afternoon. I'm from the lab. Just here to draw some blood."

"Yes. Thank you." Dr. Baker turned to Beth and Stephen. "They have to do a lot of testing before the transfusion, so I'm going to get out of her way."

Beth let go of Ali's hand and grabbed the doctor's. "Dr. Baker."

"Jess."

"Jess, would you mind explaining everything to Ali? It's just so complicated, and she'll have a lot of questions I know I won't be able to answer."

"Of course." She said to Alison, "Why don't we step outside and we can talk over in the waiting area?"

Beth eyed the needle being prepared with something akin to terror. She'd always been afraid of needles. Sometimes she even cried when she had blood drawn, or so she said. These days she preferred to lose her dignity not with Alison but only in the presence of her husband, so Alison couldn't be sure. Stephen gave her a friendly wave and she followed Dr. Baker down the hall.

Waiting area was something of a grand name for the space. It was just an alcove with a couple of faded chairs jammed inside. She sat heavily in one of them, wanting to be back in Beth's room talking to her instead of a stranger with a fauxhawk.

Dr. Baker sat down facing her. "Where should we start? How much do you know about Beth's pregnancy issues?"

'Issues' was not exactly the word Alison expected from a doctor about her friend's medical state. Her reply had a snap to it.

"I know she has a healthy daughter, but she's had three miscarriages in the last two years. I know all of them were caused by her blood attacking the babies' blood. For some reason Rhogam doesn't help even though that's what it is supposed to do. I know she's been to five different doctors at three other hospitals and the last one told her she should just stop trying. And I know if you tell her that, you should prepare for her to get up and walk out of that room right now."

Dr. Baker laughed and sat back in her chair. "Well I won't tell her that. At least not yet." She looked thoughtful for a moment before continuing, "I guess I should start by telling you why Rhogam isn't helping her. Rhogam is a drug used for mothers whose Rh blood types don't match their baby's. Most people know blood types as their ABO type and their Rh type. For instance, my blood type is A positive. That means my ABO type is A and my Rh type is positive. Positive means Rh is present, negative means it isn't. Follow me so far?"

Alison nodded.

"Beth is type B negative. Rh is not present in her blood, so her body will see Rh positive blood as foreign."

"Exactly, so her blood can attack the baby's because they're different."

"Yes it can." Alison started to interrupt. She knew all of this, but Dr. Baker continued.

"Beth gives the baby blood while he is in the womb, and it sees his different blood. Her blood destroys his. That's called hemolysis and it creates two big problems. The first is that baby doesn't have enough blood to deliver oxygen and, second, the stuff inside a red blood cell is toxic if it gets out. When mom's blood attacks baby's blood we call it Hemolytic Disease of the Fetus or Newborn, and it can cause a miscarriage."

Alison finally got her chance to speak. "Right, but that's not what's happening here. If it was, Rhogam would stop it."

"Not necessarily. Rhogam isn't perfect. It's a drug. Like any drug, it doesn't work on everyone. The last couple of doctors Beth went to believed that was the issue. That it wasn't working because she's unlucky. They were wrong. The issue here is not from Rh type, it's from a different blood type. The mechanism is the same, but the culprit is different."

Dr. Baker sat forward and spoke faster, warming to her explanation. "Most people think we have ABO and Rh and that's it, but we actually have dozens of other blood groups. Almost everyone will go through life not knowing about them because they don't usually affect us. The problem for Beth is not that she is Rh negative, but that she is Kell negative."

"What is Kell?"

"Kell is another blood group. It works pretty much the same way Rh does. When a Kell negative mom has a baby with a Kell positive dad, there is the same danger of mismatched blood types as there is with Rh type."

Alison tried to wrap her head around the new information. "Stephen is Kell positive?"

"He is. In fact, he's a very rare type of Kell positive. It's called the McLeod phenotype and it doesn't always show up in standard testing." She sat back again and sighed, sounding defeated. "After her last miscarriage, Beth showed a strong reaction to Kell so they checked Steve. It didn't show up. I ordered the McLeod testing on a hunch and he has the markers for it."

"Is that bad for him?"

"Not my area of expertise." She moved on a little too quickly for Alison's liking. "It wasn't good for Ann Boleyn. It's what got her killed."

Alison squinted. "That's not true. Ann Boleyn didn't die from some blood thing. With all due respect, I'm a professor of history. Ann Boleyn was beheaded by her husband Henry VIII."

It seemed impossible to wipe the smile off this woman's face. She didn't look at all perturbed by Alison correcting her. Instead, she laughed and said, "Very true. He beheaded her because she couldn't provide him with a male heir. She had a daughter and then a string of miscarriages. He had her beheaded and tried for a son with Jane Seymour. Actually, all of his wives had issues with miscarriages. It's just that Ann was the only one who got the chop for it. In any case, the evidence suggests he had McLeod and that's why she kept miscarrying. So, it *is* what got her killed."

Alison disliked the semantics of the argument, but the doctor's knowledge impressed her enough to keep her silent.

"Enough history. What's important right now is that Beth is going to have a hard time carrying any pregnancy to term. Her body is really good at attacking the Kell positive cells, and it is not something we can shut off. There is no Rhogam-type drug for it, so we have to treat the little guy's HDFN."

"And how are you planning to do that?"

"Aggressively." She was all business again, the neutral expression firmly back in place. "For a start, Beth is on bed rest for the remainder of her pregnancy. It's a significant period of time, but studies have shown that women on bed rest fare better in these cases. Second, we are going to have to take him early. I was hoping to get him to thirty-two weeks, but that is best-case scenario. Until we can deliver we focus on treatment through intrauterine exchange transfusions."

The world slipped in a little at the edges as Alison focused on her words. "And what is that?"

"It's a procedure that exchanges his blood, which Beth's is attacking, with blood that she won't attack. The problem, of course, is that he can't exactly provide us with an IV site while he's still in the womb. We use ultrasound to locate the umbilical vein, the main vein in the umbilical cord. We pass a needle through Beth's abdomen, through the placenta and into the umbilical cord. When we hit that we pump in the good blood and hers backs off."

Alison's own blood thumped in her ears. It didn't take medical knowledge to understand all of the ways that could go seriously wrong. The thought was terrifying.

Dr. Baker could see the fear in her eyes. "It sounds scary, I know."

"It sounds insane!"

"It's not that bad. And each time it gets easier."

"Each time?" Alison stood, her anxiety compelling her legs to move. "How often do you have to do this?"

"As often as it takes. As long as the procedure remains safe. Problems can arise if we puncture the placenta too often. We'll limit it to not more than once every week or two until we can deliver."

"Once a week!" She walked to the other end of the hall, wrapped her arms around her stomach and walked back. Dr. Baker hadn't moved. "Will it work?"

"It's the best chance he's got."

"Will it work?"

Dr. Baker stood and faced her, her eyes full of regret. "I can't answer that question. Not yet. I wish this were a TV show where I could tell you there will be a happy ending. I want their son to live. I want him to meet his sister. To play baseball and go trick-or-treating. Beth wants that too. She is strong and optimistic and, believe it or not, that helps. I can't give you odds and I can't give you promises. But if we don't do this, I can tell you with a great deal of certainty what will happen."

Tears filled Alison's eyes and she looked away, gritting her teeth against them. She nodded and Dr. Baker took the hint, walking back to the nurses station. Alison stared at the chair she had been sitting in until her eyes were dry and she felt like she could go back into her best friend's hospital room without losing her composure. It took a very long time.

CHAPTER TWO

When Alison stepped back through the sliding doors into the sunshine, the streets of Richmond were buzzing with life. It was just after five o'clock. Businessmen and politicians heading home for dinner packed the sidewalks. She slipped into the crowd and immediately wished she hadn't. She fell in step next to a tall, slim man wearing a three-piece suit and a leather messenger bag strapped across his chest, shouting into his cell phone. The crowd was too thick for her to step away from him, so she was forced, for the second time today, to deal with someone who annoyed her.

The State Capitol was just a block to the left, its emerald lawns and snow-white columns hidden by the façades of commerce, every other nearby building of the high-rise corporate office variety. Richmond's downtown was a thriving business district and distinct from the other, more residential or cultural areas. The man walking beside Alison, yammering into his cell phone as if everyone else on the street cared what he had to say, was typical of the breed that plagued this part of the city.

Nearly every aspect of his appearance was a mark against him in Alison's eyes. To start with, his suit fit too well. A well-tailored suit suggested a vanity she found particularly distasteful in men. Then to wear a messenger bag strapped across the chest of a suit he paid so much for was simply ridiculous. The suit cost more than his monthly mortgage payment. The bag was sure to destroy his jacket.

Then there was the massive, chunky watch that dangled loosely on his wrist. He'd spent hundreds of dollars on a watch and didn't have the extra links taken out of the band. It suggested the casual sloppiness of wealth and privilege. It reminded Alison of her dad, who cared only about how to buy things, not how to maintain them. A car passed close to her, and the gust of wind sent a burst of the man's cologne toward her. It was a sharp, chemical smell and he wore far too much of it. He let loose an obnoxious laugh at something he'd heard on his phone. The sharp pain that shot through Alison's jaw was the only reason she stopped clenching her teeth. She hated people who laughed too loud. Mercifully, he turned down the next street and left her in relative peace. She focused on the city rather than the people in an attempt to relax.

The skyline of Richmond, Virginia had changed drastically in the decades that Alison lived here. It had become a lovely, complex mixture of the old and the new. Alison passed the new City Hall, a towering steel and glass structure that exuded modern confidence, and glanced across the busy street at the rugged stone exterior of Old City Hall. The building sat in stark contrast to the towers around it, and yet its dignity was unmistakable. The roughly carved gray stone was a testament to the deep roots of this place, the longevity and solidity that its existence represented mortared together and solid as the day it was first built. Alison loved how Richmond was constantly blending the old and the new, and most of that was due to the college whose hospital she had just left.

Virginia Commonwealth University had garnered some national fame in recent years thanks to the success of its men's basketball team, but the real impact of the school was written in the skyline. The college had existed in some form or another in the center of this city for almost two hundred years. Since its inception, the medical college earned VCU its highest praise. As Alison turned with the majority of the crowd around her onto 8th Street, she wondered how many of them still called the hospital MCV, or Medical College of Virginia, as she did. The name had changed to VCU Medical Center around the turn of the 21st century, but these were a people famous for their reluctance to release the past. Whatever name people used, the hospital helped provide the funds to revitalize Richmond's once struggling downtown.

The nineties had not been easy on the city. She'd witnessed it with the eyes of a teenager, and so hadn't found the names for what happened to her beloved city until later. Recession and suburban flight had hit the downtown businesses hard. They shuttered their doors and jobs dried up. Crime soared and the homicide rate was staggering. Given the environment, most businesses fled to the surrounding counties along with their employees. The men in power suits surrounding her on the sidewalk had probably worked in office parks thirty miles west when they started their careers. Her father had been one of the lucky few who stayed, so Alison got to stay too.

Meanwhile, VCU quietly and cheaply bought up block after block of the decaying city. They ripped down old buildings and replaced them with shiny new classrooms, dorms and art galleries. With each new structure came new jobs, new income, and slowly but surely the recovery crept along. Residents had mixed feelings about the bulldozing, but their city flourished with its new face. Alison's feelings were mixed too, so many historical places decimated, but her city was beautiful again. A new type of beautiful, but beautiful nonetheless. Love them or hate them for it, VCU had cleaned the place up. Corporations decided Richmond was worth taking a chance on again.

The crowd around her peeled off with each parking deck they passed, and the young began to mix among the old guard. Students from the medical college were leaving classes, heading for the shuttles that would take them to classes or coffee shops on the other side of campus. Alison arrived at a shuttle stop just in time to hop on with them. She scanned the card identifying her as a professor and entitling her to a free ride back to her side of campus. If traffic was fair, she would make it back in time to teach her last class of the day, a graduate seminar that should provide the academic distraction she craved.

VCU split its campus and its focus roughly evenly between medical education facilities downtown and the main campus a few miles west in The Fan and Museum Districts. Alison felt her comfort level rising with each block they traveled. As the shuttle left the medical college behind, it also left the world of wealth and privilege. The students on the medical side of campus tended to be clean-cut, exactly what you would expect from the next generation of doctors, dentists and nurses. The other side of Virginia Commonwealth was predominantly an arts college. Some of the arts were liberal, like the history classes she taught, but most were visual. The students there were more likely to have tattoos on their arms, piercings in their noses and paint stains on their jeans. Still, the campuses mixed freely, and she saw a good number of khakis mixed amongst the artfully ripped T-shirts as the bus slowed and dropped her off outside the Hibbs Building.

At a fresh-looking thirty-five years of age, Alison was young to judge too harshly, but still she had to hold back from rolling her eyes at some of the scene around her. She had never been the type to live too wild a life. She'd grown up on the wealthy side of middle class, and her parents made sure she and her two sisters wanted for nothing. They'd all gone to the best schools and were given every opportunity to succeed. Inevitably, her oldest sister left home in rebellion and her middle sister also resented the perceived interference of their parents. Being the youngest, Alison had the perspective to see her parents' generosity and felt bound to honor it. The upshot was that though she lived a full, happy life, she'd never had time for wild and crazy. These kids knew nothing else. Half of them still looked hungover as they headed to dinner.

She pushed past a crowd of students leaving Hibbs and heading across the brick paved courtyard to the dining center directly opposite. This group was more her style. She recognized more than one student's face and guessed they were, if not history majors, probably business or engineering. Something more intellectual and less dirty than artists. She may teach non-majors most of the time, but she was an academic and felt she fit the part. Her wardrobe was heavy on long, flowing skirts, tight-cabled sweaters and cotton blouses. When she branched out to wear slacks, she usually paired them with loafers. She made an effort to stay closer to the modern hippie look than, say, the uptight librarian, and succeeded more days than she failed.

Alison pushed through the door to her classroom just as the first students were arriving. As she settled herself at the teacher's desk, her phone buzzed. It was a text message from Beth.

Stop worrying. Everything is going to be fine. Have a good class! See you tomorrow!

At least Beth still had optimism. After living this same nightmare with her best friend so many times, Alison felt like her store was completely empty.

CHAPTER THREE

Stepping into the hallway, Alison pulled the door to Beth's room shut behind her, careful to hold the handle down until it eased into the frame, pleased to hear only the faintest click. Beth had dropped off to sleep while they were chatting, and Alison didn't want to wake her. She'd gone through a long afternoon of tests and waiting on tenterhooks. Alison wanted to be sure that she got enough rest.

"How's our girl?"

Dr. Baker stood at the nurses station, scribbling a note into a green binder.

"I beg your pardon?"

Dr. Baker finished writing with a flourish and clicked her pen. She looked up with a warm smile. "Beth. How is she?"

"Haven't you seen her today?"

She flipped the lid of the binder shut and dropped it onto the desk behind the counter. "Yes. I'm sure she told you everything went well in the OR this morning. I was with her until around noon when they moved her to the recovery room."

"So you know how she is."

She folded her arms and leaned against the counter. "There are things a patient will tell their family that she won't tell her doctor."

"We aren't family."

"That's not how Beth and Stephen see it. Didn't Stephen say that everything in their house goes through you?"

"Stephen is very proud of his little joke." Alison shifted her bag a little higher on her shoulder. "I'm surprised you remember."

"I'm a good listener."

"I'm sure." She peered down the hall, which was empty and quiet despite all of the occupied rooms. "Beth's fine."

"Glad to hear it. How are you?"

"Me? Why do you ask?"

"Because a high risk pregnancy is not an easy thing to deal with." She pushed off the counter and stood straight as a rail. "It's hard for mom and baby, but it's just as hard for the family. It's common to feel helpless and scared, but also like you're not allowed to share it. I wanted to make sure you were okay."

It occurred to Alison that Dr. Baker had seen how upset she was yesterday and must now think she was fragile. Or too involved in her friend's life. "I'm fine."

"You and Beth seem very close."

Too involved, then. "We've been friends a long time."

She was playing with the pen between her long fingers, clicking it open and shut. "It's good that she has that kind of support. Beth is very special."

Emotion piled up in Alison's throat, and she swallowed hard against it. "Yes she is."

"How did you meet?" She finally held the pen still. "If you don't mind my asking."

She did mind. She did not want to talk to this woman. She wanted to be at home on her couch with a very large glass of wine and a very soft pair of pajamas, but she felt the need to advocate for Beth.

"In Sunday school when we were too young to notice any differences between us. When we were old enough to notice, there weren't any differences anymore."

"That's a lovely way of putting it." She clipped the pen on her breast pocket and stuffed her hands into the pockets of her jeans. "So you've been friends ever since?"

"Ever since."

"That's rare. I don't think I can even remember the names of anyone I met so young."

Alison checked the hall again, it was still empty. "Yes, well, Beth isn't easy to forget."

"I can believe that." Alison was raising her wrist to look at her watch, preparing her escape line, when Dr. Baker said suddenly, "What's your number?"

"Excuse me?"

She pulled her phone from her lab coat, activating the screen as she spoke. "Your cell phone number. What is it? I have some links to some articles I want to send you."

Alison pulled her phone from her purse, confusion more than anything else forcing her to comply. She brought up her number from the menu and handed the phone to Dr. Baker.

She handed it back almost immediately, typing furiously as she explained, "They're just some websites that deal with Kell blood type and HDFN associated with it. I already gave them to Beth and Stephen. I thought you might want to check them out. You seem the sort who needs more information than I gave you yesterday. There's not much medical jargon in them. I just thought it might help put your mind at ease to know more."

Alison's phone buzzed as she dropped it back into her purse. "Thank you."

"Of course."

She started down the hall, but stopped and turned. "It was kind of you to think of it."

"Of course."

Alison felt like there was more to say, but couldn't think what, so she continued down the hall and out of the hospital.

CHAPTER FOUR

The sun was setting over downtown by the time Alison made it to the hospital the next day. As the sliding glass doors ticked open she was able to see, over the heads of the considerable crowd, the blond monolith that was Stephen. He was on his cell phone, pacing back and forth behind a pair of chairs in the lobby. His usual lazy smile carved a series of radiating lines on his heavily tanned cheeks like ripples from a stone dropped in a pond. Everything about Stephen screamed of the outdoors, from the year-round tan to the aroma of cut grass and sunshine that was as much a permanent part of him as his skin.

An older woman unwittingly stepped into the path of his pacing. She tottered for a moment from the collision, but he reached out and caught her elbow, sending her on her way with a smile to strengthen his silent apology. She smiled back, not the least upset by his carelessness. In fact, she moved with a lighter step than before. That had always been the greatest of Stephen's gifts. He could charm anyone and everyone he met even for the briefest moment.

Alison could still remember the night she and Beth met him. They had been in Boston for almost a year, but had been so busy with their studies that they rarely left their ice-cold basement apartment. When they both ended up with a Friday night off, they decided to celebrate at the bar on the corner. Its thumping music had been a siren song for weeks. The little place turned out to be everything they wanted it to be. Low lighting, polished wood, reasonable prices and a high bistro table in a corner perfect for people watching. Alison had just broken up with a sweet guy who kissed like a malfunctioning vacuum cleaner and she had no interest in replacing him any time soon. She focused entirely on finding someone for Beth, who had been single for far too long.

Beth's eyes scanned the crowd over her glass of chardonnay, and Alison noted that they kept going back to one particular table. So fixated on Beth was Stephen that he looked like he'd been punched in the face. Alison watched him for a good five minutes and swore he never blinked; he was staring at Beth so hard he didn't notice his buddy elbowing him in the ribs.

"Will you go talk to that guy before he passes out? He looks seven feet tall at least. He'll break something when he falls down."

"What are you talking about? What guy?"

"The one you can't keep your eyes off of." Alison waved at him and he finally seemed to notice her next to Beth. "He's been drooling into his beer since we walked in."

He stood up.

"Don't wave at him! Why did you do that? Now he's coming over here!"

"Exactly! You're welcome."

He didn't even spare Alison a glance before introducing himself to Beth. Neither of them noticed when she wandered off to the bar a few minutes after he sat down.

The next day when he called to ask Beth out to dinner she accepted, but almost immediately decided to cancel. She came up with a dozen excuses why she couldn't go out with him and left Alison to say the real reason out loud.

"You aren't canceling because you don't like him. You're canceling because you're afraid you do like him. You think you're probably going to fall for this white guy."

Beth was less than willing to admit the truth, but Alison knew her too well to be fooled. She also knew better than to back down. So she pushed when Beth pulled and waited for her to accept the inevitable. When Beth grabbed the phone to actually cancel the date, Alison yanked the cord from the wall so hard that a little chunk of plaster came loose and rattled to the floor.

"Damn it Beth! You are going to go on that date!"

"Why do you care so much if I go out with this guy?"

"Because he's perfect for you!" She brandished the frayed end of the phone cord at Beth in a way that would have been funny if the moment hadn't been so emotionally charged. "Because he's perfect and you have terrible taste in men. Because it doesn't matter that he's white, it matters that he makes you smile. And since you aren't likely to find another decent guy any time soon, you're going to go out with this one. You're going to let yourself fall in love. I wanna dance at your wedding, Beth."

That hadn't ended the fight, but Alison had broken the phone so Beth couldn't cancel the date. That one date was all it took. Alison danced at their wedding a few years later.

Watching him now, still alight with happiness despite the fact that his wife was essentially chained to a hospital bed for the foreseeable future and the baby she was carrying needed constant monitoring, she wondered if she had judged him a little too kindly back then. Alison shook herself, aware that fear and annoyance were erasing her charity.

Stephen turned again and this time he spotted Alison. He waved and ended the call.

"Ali!"

"Hello, Stephen. How's Beth?"

"Good. I was just heading out to pick Rachel up for dinner."

She knew from experience that he wasn't likely to say more about Beth's condition. He deferred to the doctors when it came to Beth's health, and Alison had learned that pressing him was a waste of breath. She would have to get her information from the source. Right now, she had other concerns.

"Stephen, there's something I wanted to talk to you about."

"Uh-oh." An exaggerated look of concern almost settled into place before his smile ruined it. "This sounds serious."

"It is. I want to know more about this blood thing that you have."

"The McLeod thing." He waved his hand and the smile lines in his cheeks deepened. "It's not a big deal."

"You know, that's what Beth's doctor said too. The more I hear it, the less I believe it." He didn't offer up any information, so she continued, "I'm not letting it go, Stephen. How dangerous is this?"

"It's not dangerous, Ali." Staring into his eyes, she didn't budge from where she stood. "Okay fine. If I tell you what I know will you let me go pick up my daughter?"

"I'll consider it."

"Fair enough," he said with a deep chuckle. "So it's a hereditary disorder called McLeod Syndrome. The same thing that gives me the Kell blood type causes it."

"What does that mean? Is it a mutation or something?"

"I guess so." He held up his hand at the look she gave him. "I'm not avoiding the question, I just don't exactly understand. It's sorta sciencey. There's a specialist I'm going to see once life goes back to normal. All I really know is it can cause some issues later on."

"What kind of issues?"

"Anemia, muscle pain, heart problems, and what one of the articles Jess gave me to read charmingly called 'behavioral changes.' Bottom line is my heart will give out at about the same time I go crazy."

"Stephen, that's not funny."

"No it isn't, but there's nothing I can do about it."

"Wait, you're serious?"

"Yep. I might have a mild version of it with no problems at all. I might have a severe case and die five years after I develop symptoms, there's no way to tell."

"They can't tell you how bad it is?"

"Nope. I just have to wait and see. I can drink my milk and eat my spinach, and it'll still happen. So I'm just not going to worry about it."

"Stephen…"

"Ali, look…" He sighed, glancing over her shoulder at the sliding glass doors and the sidewalk beyond them. "The articles said symptoms will appear in my fifties. I have twenty years before I have to worry about this thing. I'm not going to drive myself crazy."

"Have you made an appointment with the specialist?"

"I already have a nagging wife to hassle me about that."

"Have you made an appointment with the specialist?"

He put a hand heavily on her shoulder. "I promised Beth I'll make an appointment as soon as she's out of here with our son."

Alison bit back the words she wanted to fling at him about his optimism. "Fine. Just know there will be two of us holding you to that."

He laughed so loud a few people turned to look at him. Using the hand on her shoulder, he pulled her into a bone-crushing hug. The smell of grass and sunshine was there, but the antiseptic smells of the hospital nearly covered them. The mixture made Alison's stomach turn. She wrapped her arms around his thick waist and held on tight. Part of her hoped that she could squeeze some of that positivity out for herself. But when she headed for the elevator, she didn't feel any better.

CHAPTER FIVE

Alison sat in a university faculty meeting in rising impatience with her current lot in life. Most people were surprised to hear that the vast majority of a college professor's working time was spent outside the classroom. Writing lesson plans, composing tests, grading and counseling students filled countless hours. Then there was the time she had to spend on her own research, writing and publications. When all of that was taken into account, class time, the fun part as Alison thought of it, represented just a small fraction of what she did. Everything else was the busy work of the academic and the most tedious of those time-consuming tasks, as far as Alison was concerned, were faculty meetings.

Their ostensible purpose, she'd been told, was to keep all faculty abreast of each other's work and the happenings of the college. In reality the meetings devolved into either an hour of bragging, like this one, or an hour and a half of complaining. Alison's friends in the corporate world assured her this was not exclusive to academia. One in particular, who had spent nearly two decades in the banking industry, insisted that she had never once attended a meeting that could not just as easily have been an email. Of course, she generally said this after she'd had so many vodka and Red Bulls that she was grabbing the waiter's butt every time he walked by, so Alison took her words with a grain of salt. Still, the reality of staff meetings as a waste of time seemed to be universally accepted by everyone except those who conducted them.

This one marked the end of her day. She had prepared everything for the next day's classes and even locked her office before arriving here in the conference room. The droning, inconsequential voices of her colleagues were keeping her from going to check on Beth after her second procedure that afternoon.

Just as Dr. Baker had predicted, a week after being admitted Beth was back in the operating room. Beth texted at lunchtime to say everything had gone well, but the fact that she had been transfused again reminded Alison that this doctor's dangerous solution had not fixed anything the first time.

She stared at her clasped hands, chasing one worry after another through her mind and completely ignoring the words floating in the air around her. Her colleagues were all brilliant scholars, but as more time ticked by she couldn't help hating them for their long-winded intellect. She tuned into the conversation long enough to hear Dr. Alfredson, the department chair, tell a truly awful joke involving a reference librarian and a mathematician. He was a gifted historian, approximately as wide as he was tall and with significantly more hair on his chin than his head. Comedy was not his forte. He started to laugh with a wheezing sort of whine just loud enough to cover the fact that no one else joined him.

When he finally caught his breath, he sighed and said, "Well, my distinguished ladies and gentlemen, I do believe that concludes our business for today."

Alison grabbed her papers and shoved them into her bag.

"Unless anyone has any concerns they would care to address before we adjourn for the evening?"

Knowing she would be unable to stop herself from looking daggers at anyone who raised their hand, Alison sat still and stared at the worn clasp on her briefcase.

"No? Well then, until we meet again."

She was on her feet and to the door before anyone else moved. She wrenched the door open and took exactly three steps when she heard her name.

"Hey Alison!"

She turned to see one of her teaching assistants making her way down the hall. Jennifer was the doctoral candidate Alison was advising, teaching assistant in nearly all of her classes and, though she hadn't expected it when they first met, a good friend. One of the things Alison liked best about Jennifer was that she was quick enough to take excellent notes in all their shared classes. It was why Alison insisted she be there, tucked away in the front corner of the classroom, every time Alison taught. Unfortunately, that quickness didn't seem to translate to her pace outside the classroom. At the moment she was walking so slowly Alison could have screamed.

"You were sure bookin' it out of here. Got a date?"

Alison forced a smile, but kept her body angled toward the staircase. "No. My friend is in the hospital and I need to go see her."

"Oh, I'm sorry. Not Beth again? Is she still having trouble getting pregnant?"

"She doesn't have trouble getting pregnant. She has trouble staying pregnant."

"Okay. I won't keep you. I wanted to let you know that Courtney and I are going out for a drink later and we want you to come. It sounds like you could use the distraction, so I'll just assume your answer is yes. We'll pick you up at ten."

"I'm not sure I can make it."

"Of course you can."

"Dr. Reynolds." She jumped at the booming voice of her boss. "I am pleased to have caught up with you, Dr. Reynolds." He squinted in Jennifer's direction, his jaw hanging slack for a moment. Eventually he realized he had no idea what her name was, so he turned back to Alison. "You appeared less than attentive in our faculty meeting, Dr. Reynolds."

Whether it was his extreme age or his normal manner Alison wasn't sure, but Dr. Alfredson had the habit of continuously repeating her name during their conversations. Several professors pointed out that he did this almost exclusively with the female faculty. They took it as a sign that he didn't think a woman was capable of remembering her own name. Alison preferred to think of it as a charming eccentricity. Or, more likely, that he wasn't capable of remembering who he was speaking to for more than a minute.

"I apologize, Dr. Alfredson. My friend was admitted into the hospital recently. I'm a bit distracted."

He smiled and waggled his finger shockingly close to her nose. "Now, now Dr. Reynolds. I doubt you would accept such a flimsy excuse from one of your students if he were to underperform." He gave a closed mouth smile that pushed his cheeks up over the majority of his eyes. "Indeed, imagine if Henry V had paid such scant attention at Agincourt! What may have befallen his band of brothers then?"

Jennifer's voice was just above a whisper. "More importantly, what may have befallen the career of Kenneth Branaugh?"

"Beg pardon, my dear? I didn't quite catch that."

"She was agreeing with you, sir." Alison smiled as widely as she could force her mouth. "You're right. I should do better. I'll be more attentive at our next meeting."

"Well. Yes. See that you are, Dr. Reynolds. Good day to you both."

As he turned to walk away, something he said sparked her memory. She reached out and grabbed his meaty arm. "Dr. Alfredson! I have a question for you before you go. If you have time."

He looked down his nose at her hand and answered, "I always have time for my staff, Dr. Reynolds."

"Thank you, sir. I heard a...I suppose a theory about Henry VIII."

"Henry Tudor? Bit outside your time period, is he not?"

"He is. That's why I wanted to ask you. I thought you may be familiar with the facts."

He tucked his thumb under the strap of his suspenders and preened. All he needed was a thick cigar and he could have been mistaken for Churchill. No doubt that was his intention.

"Do go on."

"I heard he had some sort of blood disorder that prevented his wives from providing him an heir."

"Ah, yes. I've heard something about that." He paused, staring at the ceiling. Jennifer covered her smile with her hand. "I forget the name, Dr. Reynolds. Something Scottish if I'm not much mistaken. Somewhat ironic. In any case, I have heard the theory. The DNA in his blood or some such thing caused his wives to miscarry after their first child. Unluckily, they had girls and not the son he wanted. Seems rather convenient. For the researchers, mind, not the wives. Rather inconvenient for the wives."

"Is that the only evidence? His wives miscarried and so this had to be the cause?"

"There is apparently some sort of physical change associated with the condition, Dr. Reynolds." Each time he used her title she twitched, but she had never found a professional way of telling him she disliked it. "I believe the blood syndrome is used to explain his foul temper and rapidly declining health."

"His heart gave out around the same time he went crazy."

"I dislike the flippancy of your tone. We are discussing one of the greatest kings England has ever known."

Dr. Alfredson had an infamous dislike of fidgeting, so Alison contented herself with digging her fingernails into her palm to relieve her annoyance. "But is it a valid theory?"

He looked down his nose at her again, this time allowing his lip to curl ever so slightly. "Quite the reverse. There is not a shred of evidence to support it, and evidence cannot ever be found, given the limits of science."

Perhaps it was the way he said "science" the way most people say "pedophile" that caused Jennifer to throw her shoulders back and remark, "A lack of evidence doesn't necessarily mean the theory is invalid."

He turned to her with simpering dislike. "My dear girl, when you have been in the field of history as long as I, you find that there are as many crackpot theories as there are stars in the night sky. Our field requires, if not empirical evidence, at the very least anecdotal evidence. This fantasy has neither."

Rather than allowing one of her favorite students to ruin her career before it started, Alison stepped between the two. "Thank you so much. I didn't think much of the idea. It came from an unreliable source. I appreciate your time, Professor."

With one last cutting look at Jennifer, he nodded and stalked off.

"He should be stuffed and mounted in a museum." Jennifer turned back to Alison. "What was that all about?"

"Nothing." She was about to make for the stairs but stopped. "He's right, you know. About needing evidence to support our assertions. Keep that in mind when you prepare your dissertation. I've seen more than one colleague fall in love with a theory and refuse to give it up even when they couldn't support it."

"Yeah. I know. Just because he's right doesn't mean he isn't a condescending old windbag."

Alison checked her watch and swore, heading for the stairs.

Jennifer called down the hall, "Ten o'clock! Outside your apartment!"

CHAPTER SIX

Beth was fast asleep when Alison arrived at her hospital door. She pulled the visitor's chair a little closer and sat as quietly as she could. Beth's pencil-thin dreadlocks, which reached to the middle of her back when she stood, spread across her nest of pillows. Alison remembered when Beth started growing them. They were thirteen years old, both sprawled across the hand-sewn quilt that covered Beth's twin bed. Their heads were bent over their textbooks, studying for a history test, and both of them were constantly tucking their artificially straightened hair behind their ears. Finally, Alison pulled her hair back and twisted it into a sloppy braid and was back at work. Beth made a huffy noise and said that she wished her hair was that easy to manage. She decided on the spot that she was going to twist her hair into dreadlocks. Alison had no idea what that meant, and Beth teased her for being a "sheltered little white girl."

They spent years wasting every spare moment they could watching movies, gossiping and gushing over boys and later, for Alison's benefit, girls. Every moment of that time Beth was twisting her hair to keep her locks tight. When they both aced their SATs, when they had their first drinks, when they had their first heartbreaks. Delicate fingers twisting that hair accompanied every tear and every smile. The movement had become calming to Alison. Her piece of normal. She resisted the urge to shake Beth awake and beg her to twist her dreadlocks.

If Alison and Beth had cemented a friendship early on, the path their relationship had taken was a twisting one. Alison was outgoing and made lots of friends. At heart, though, she was more of an introvert. She kept all of her friends in the shallow end of her life, letting them in only so far. She had always been that way, keeping everything superficial, but Beth simply wouldn't have it. She was the first person who ever called Alison out on the veneer of her friendships. Before they were even out of elementary school, she turned on Alison, who was trying to shake her off to go home alone and read, and told her in no uncertain terms that they were going to be best friends and Alison was just going to have to get used to it. Beth ended up going over to her house that day and nearly every day after until they moved in to their shared UR dorm room, and she didn't have to bully her way to an invitation.

Alison, for her part, was secretly thrilled that someone worked so hard to be close to her. She was the youngest in a family of five living in a world designed for families of four. Somehow, she was always forgotten or pushed aside. She slept on the rollout cot in hotel rooms. She had to perch on the edge of the seat in the too-small restaurant booth. She got hand-me-down clothes and no one remembered that she liked sausage instead of pepperoni on her pizza. Her parents had only so much time and interest to devote to their children, and her sisters were both loud, opinionated and demanded attention.

Alison demanded nothing, and so she got nothing. Beth knew. Beth ordered a small sausage pie for them in Pizza Hut. Beth took her to another table to sit when the booth was full and her sisters took all eyes away from her. Beth slept on the floor with her, gossiping all night long. Beth gave her the confidence to expect more. But Beth also gave her space when she needed it. She was, quite simply, the perfect best friend for an awkward adolescent trying to find herself.

Then Alison nearly fell flat on her face the first day of Spanish class junior year of high school. The new teacher, Ms. Fields, was a young, redheaded hippie with long braids and a thousand necklaces that clinked as she paced the room, quizzing them on conjugations. Alison watched her until her eyes watered and then watched her some more. She heard the woman's voice ringing in her ears when she lay down to sleep at night. She became oddly vocal about how Spanish was her favorite class. She made grand plans to hitchhike through Andalusia after graduation.

A month into the semester Beth called her out. They were sitting in her bedroom one afternoon. She was piling on the leather chokers and cheap chains she had bought at the mall.

Beth looked at her stonily and said, "You know you're totally gay right?"

She scoffed and denied it and even got mad at Beth, yelling at her as she never had in all the years they'd known each other. Beth sat quietly and waited for her to stop. Then she said that she thought it was totally cool and she loved Ali to pieces, but that she needed to chill with Ms. Fields because it was totally *not* cool to crush on a teacher. Alison denied it and yelled more and Beth was sweet and patient and never stopped supporting her.

When Beth went home Alison sat on her bed and wondered what Ms. Fields was doing right then. She realized, with a blistering clarity, that Beth was right. She was totally gay. The next day she faked sick so she didn't have to go to school, and Beth showed up around lunchtime with the sickly sweet french vanilla lattes they would drink and pretend to be grownups. She held Alison while she cried and then told her to stop crying because there was nothing at all wrong with being gay.

Because Beth could convince her of anything in those days, Alison believed her. She believed that it was okay to be gay. She believed it right up until she met Billy Edwards, a pitcher for the St. Christopher's baseball team who made her completely forget about Ms. Fields. She tossed the cheap necklaces into her new Chicago Cubs trash can and started lecturing Beth on the pristine beauty that was the slider and the quirkiness of the knuckleball. She announced to Beth that she wasn't gay after all, and Beth smiled and shook her head and then she was yelling at Beth again. Using words about herself like "phase" and "experiment." Beth sat back, smiled, and told her she would figure it out eventually.

"Eventually" came sometime between the backseat of Billy's Jetta and the makeup room with the busty blond captain of the show choir. Neither had exactly made her toes curl, but each had helped her realize that not everything in life is black and white. The smug smile on Beth's face was infuriating, but Alison had the perspective to see that her friendship was an enigma in the mid-nineties American South.

She saw the way people reacted to Ellen's "Yep, I'm gay" announcement, had noted that her local station refused to air the TV episode. She watched news crews descend on Laramie, Wyoming and she shed tears for Matthew Shepard though she was one of few in town who did. Having Beth as her best friend made it so easy to come out. Beth never judged her, and she wouldn't let Alison hate herself, even when she wanted to. Beth's friendship was special. She was grateful for it beyond words and it was those moments, even more than the toothless grin of a four-year-old, that made her completely devoted to her best friend.

Devoted enough to stand between her and knuckle-dragging racists that were dotted throughout their hometown. Devoted enough to convince her, with the same knowing smile through Beth's own storm of shouting, to go on that date even though the ridiculously cute guy was white. Devoted enough to not just accept but to celebrate her marrying that ridiculously cute white guy. Devoted enough to hold her while she curled up in the fetal position sobbing over another miscarriage. Devoted enough to encourage her to keep trying when she secretly thought Beth and Stephen would never have another baby.

So here she found herself, rapidly approaching forty, with this one best friend and little else. She had a rented apartment, a leased car and a non-tenured position at the college. But she had Beth.

A cart with a bad wheel banged by in the hallway just outside the door and both women jumped. Beth's forehead furrowed and she blinked lazily. When she finally focused on the face in front of her, her mouth split into a familiar grin.

"Ali!" She struggled to push herself into a sitting position. "How long have you been sitting there? You should have woken me up."

Alison smiled and took the hand Beth offered. "Nah, you need your rest. How did everything go?"

Beth yawned and the fingers of her free hand went to her scalp, feeling for the base of one of her dreadlocks. Alison's shoulders relaxed. "I told you it went fine. Jess was able to give him more blood than she planned on."

Alison made a face. She'd had time to think over everything, and she had an uneasy feeling about this pregnancy. She worried that not only the baby but also Beth were in danger from this procedure. Fear ate at her all night, every night, and she barely slept. It felt to Alison like this Dr. Baker was just so proud of herself for solving the mystery of the miscarriages that she was prolonging the inevitable. Maybe she wanted to write the case up for a journal. Maybe she wanted to show off to her new boss. Whatever was driving her, Beth would be the one to suffer when it failed. She had been distracted and tired all week and she blamed Dr. Baker for her mood.

Beth had known her long enough to spot the look. "What?"

"Nothing. How are you feeling? You look tired."

"I *feel* tired! I feel like I was in that operating room for days. Things were easier the second time around, though. It felt more relaxed in the OR this time. Jess even told me when Stephen was smiling at me from the gallery."

"Shouldn't she have been paying attention to the massive needle in your belly?"

"Don't remind me. Anyway it was after the whole thing was over." Beth squinted at her, her fingers moving to a new spot in her hair. "You don't like her."

Alison shrugged, but even as she did, she knew it wouldn't be enough.

"Don't shrug at me, Dr. Reynolds! What's wrong with my doctor?"

"Ugh! Don't call me Dr. Reynolds! You know I hate that!" She looked at their interlaced thumbs for a moment, but saw no way out. "There's nothing wrong with her. She's just…"

The pause drew out too long and Beth prodded her. "She's just what?"

Alison rolled her eyes, giving in as she always knew she would. "Come on! The tattoos. The hair. She looks like a barista, not a doctor!"

"Okay, so she doesn't exactly look the part."

"Doesn't look the part? That's an understatement. She looks like one of my undergrads. Or the girl who worked at the UR bookstore."

"You had a crush on the girl who worked at the UR bookstore."

"I was eighteen. I had a crush on everyone." She shifted in her chair and looked seriously at her friend. "Are you sure she's qualified?"

Beth stopped twisting her hair. "You're serious, aren't you?"

"Of course I am. I'm worried about you."

"Why didn't you say something before now?"

"I didn't want to worry you."

"So you've been biting your tongue about this for five whole days."

"Six."

"That must be a new record for you. How did you manage?"

"You've been asleep a lot."

"Funny."

"Okay, but Beth, I'm serious now."

Beth smiled in that indulgent way that mothers smile at a whiny child. "You're really sweet, Ali. I love that you're so worried about me, but I am in good hands." Alison huffed and tried to stand up, but Beth held her hand tighter and continued, "Jess is a very well respected OB. She was trained by some of the best doctors in the country and spent the last five years at Legacy Children's in Portland."

"She's from Portland?"

"Yeah. VCU worked really hard to get her here. She's supposed to be one of the marquee names for the new children's hospital they're building. If they can ever finish it." Her smile was back. "So, other than judging the book by its cover, what's wrong with her? Did she use doctor talk with you?"

"No. She didn't. And I'm not judging a book by its cover. I just…I don't know. I just don't know if I like her."

"Well you're just going to have to get used to her," Beth said, leaning back into her pillows and closing her eyes. "You're going to see a lot of her if I'm going to be in this place for two months."

Alison stood, and this time Beth let her. "Fine. I'll try. But only because you and Stephen are my favorite people in the world."

"Headed home to grade papers?"

"Yeah." She hesitated a moment. "My grad student Jennifer and her girlfriend are going to Babe's tonight. They invited me to come along but I think I'll skip it."

Beth didn't open her eyes. "No you won't. You'll go and you'll dance and you'll have a drink for me."

"I can't."

"You can and you will. I've been nursing or pregnant for the better part of the last four years. Do you know how long it's been since I've had a glass of wine?"

"Six months, fourteen days. And then it was only a 'half glass of a really disappointing chardonnay.' You and Stephen started trying again the next day and you stopped drinking just to be safe."

"Fifteen days."

"Right. Sorry. I wasn't counting today."

"So have a beer for me and have a good time."

Alison put the chair back in the corner and switched off the lights.

"Yes. ma'am."

CHAPTER SEVEN

The pound of a heavy bass line radiated from the massive speakers through Alison's skin down into her bones. She felt the thud in her marrow and moved in unison with the bodies around her, not hearing the music so much as feeling it. She closed her eyes and smiled, raising her arms above her head as she moved. The plate-glass windows behind her rattled as the chorus kicked in again.

Babe's of Carytown was either a Richmond institution or completely unknown, depending on your point of view. The bar had occupied the same dark corner in the fashionable Carytown shopping district since the days when women had to sneak in after dark to avoid being seen. The windows were tinted almost to blackness and nothing about the exterior announced that it was the city's only lesbian bar.

Times had changed dramatically since it first opened. Now it was a popular spot not only for gay women, but also for straight ones who wanted to dance without the burden of aggressive men. Whether the invasion of straight women was a good thing or a bad thing also depended on your point of view. Still, with the dwindling number of lesbian bars operating across the country, Babe's was doing well to still exist.

The interior was separated into three distinct areas. A collection of booths and a relatively quiet, if a bit divey, bar waited right next to the front door for customers. The older crowd spent their nights there, drinking and reminiscing over the good-bad old days. A little further on was the dance area, with its loud music and pool tables shoved into the back corner. The bar there was where you went to watch but not talk. The butches leaned against the pool tables and sipped their beer, always keeping at least one eye on the sweaty dancers. Past the dance floor stood a row of bathrooms that rarely held only the single occupant at a time demanded by the signs on the door. The hallway itself was dark enough to lend enough privacy for some of the goings-on. Past the bathrooms was a door to the back patio, a spacious area with yet another bar, several picnic and patio tables and a sand volleyball court.

No matter what the night of the week, these areas were predictably populated. The quiet bar for the older crowd, the dance floor for the ones who didn't want to go home alone, and the patio for the sporty types and the few holdouts who still smoked the Marlboros manufactured on the other side of a town all but synonymous with tobacco products. Times changed, but the ebb and flow of Babe's was a constant.

Alison had been coming here since she was a student at the University of Richmond. In truth, she tried to sneak in once with a fake ID when she was still at St. Catherine's. The owner, Vicki, hadn't been there to give her the lifetime ban she issued to anyone who threatened her liquor license by breaking the law. The bouncer took pity on her, sending her away with a lecture on patience. Once she hit eighteen Beth came with her because she was too timid to show up alone. They danced with black marker X's on the back of their hands until last call and laughed all the way home. She had moved to Boston and then to England, both more gay-friendly than Richmond, but the lesbian bar she loved would always be Babe's.

Tonight, since her heart was back in Beth's hospital room, she had decided to give her brain the night off too. She'd had a beer and a few shots with her friends at the loud bar, and then moved to the dance floor. She let the thump of the bass move through her like the ocean. It shuddered through her bones and eased the ache of her tense muscles. Her breathing synchronized with the beat. She danced with anyone who was around. Her thick, auburn curls caught in the sweat on her shoulders and the spaghetti straps of her tank top. Her strappy sandals occasionally smacked on the painted concrete floor.

She had no idea how long she'd been dancing, but she was thirsty and fighting to catch her breath when the music abruptly changed to a much slower beat. The revelers partnered off and a short woman with a wonderful smile wearing a red tie held out her hand to Alison. She tried to be polite when she refused, but felt a twinge of regret to watch her shrug and leave the floor. Looking around, Alison saw that she was the only person alone. She moved as quickly as the crowd would allow to the back door. Her overheated skin craved fresh air, and she guessed correctly that she would find Jennifer and Courtney on the volleyball court.

She got a beer and half-emptied it in one swig, basking in the ice-cold liquid rolling down her throat. Rather than sitting down alone, she leaned against the railing in an unoccupied corner. The patio was busy tonight. She drank the rest of her beer slowly as she looked around.

The gay community in Richmond was small enough that she usually ran into someone she knew at Babe's, but tonight she didn't see any of the usual faces. She had just drained her bottle when she felt eyes on her. Turning, she saw with a jolt of surprise Dr. Jess Baker standing in a small group across the patio looking at her with a lazy smile.

The mix of good tequila and cheap beer in Alison's blood reacted unexpectedly to her. She was wearing nearly the same outfit as when they had first met, a T-shirt and jeans, but the T-shirt was a rich cranberry color that perfectly complemented her lightly tanned skin. Her hair, which had seemed ridiculous at the hospital, in this setting was flattering to her high cheekbones and straight nose. Even the splash of color on her bicep had a different effect. Alison found herself examining the swirling shapes. One in particular caught her eye. It could have been a fish or a dragon. There were certainly scales and a sinewy body, but the overall shape was impossible to determine from this distance.

After a moment, she realized that she was staring and looked away, but she knew she was still being watched. She tipped the bottle to her lips, forgetting it was empty. Embarrassed, she looked back to find Dr. Baker gone. Her disappointment surprised her, but she shrugged it off and headed back to the bar for a new drink.

The need for alcohol seemed to have increased dramatically on the patio. The line was impossibly long for the single, harried bartender. Alison suddenly felt the heat of the dance floor on her again. She lifted the long hair off her neck, hoping the flow of air would help cool her down. The line did not move, and she shifted her weight from one foot to the other. She looked to the door that led back inside, considering going to one of the other bars for her drink. The sickly sweet strains of another love song filtered through the portal, and she thought better of it.

The line finally moved an infinitesimal amount as the person at the front stepped away, two beers in one hand, shoving bills into her pocket with the other. There was a sense of inevitability to her realization that the woman was familiar. Dr. Baker smiled and walked toward her, transferring one of the sweating bottles into her free hand.

"I didn't expect to see you here, Ms. Reynolds."

Alison dropped her hair, suddenly aware of the sweat on her brow. "Why is that, Dr. Baker?"

"Please call me Jess." She held out one of the bottles. "I didn't peg you as gay."

"I'm not. I'm bi."

"My mistake." She waved the bottle. "Close enough for me to buy you a drink, right?"

Alison looked at the line and silently debated, but whatever was in the air tonight convinced her to accept the offer. The glass was cool on her skin and she nodded her thanks.

"Wanna sit?"

The table she indicated was small, just a disk of wrought iron with a single chair on either side. Warning bells sounded in Alison's brain.

"My friends look like they're almost done with their volleyball game."

Jess looked over her shoulder just in time to see Jennifer dive for the ball, missing it by miles, but conveniently knocking Courtney into the sand beneath her. The catcalls and whistling from the crowd eventually got them back to their feet, but they took their time about it.

Jess turned back with a wink. "I don't think they're keeping score. Come on. Keep me company for a while. My friends are both busy flirting with their exes. I'm new to town and I don't know anyone else. Save this night from being a total bust?"

Her words and attitude were completely open and the genuineness won Alison over. Considering her social options were also limited, it seemed worth a chance. She chose the chair that offered her an unblocked view of the court. The minute Jennifer finished her game Alison would have an excuse to make a hasty exit.

"Beth told me everything went well this afternoon."

"It did. I can only hope it goes just as well in the future."

Alison felt the beginnings of anxiety, and fought to keep her tone light. "So you still intend to continue doing this blood exchange thing?"

"It is the best option we have."

"Have you gotten a second opinion?"

Jess smiled at her bottle. "Second opinions are something patients get independent of their physicians. Doctors will sometimes consult with each other. If you are asking if I have consulted with others about her case, the answer is yes. My training was a team-based style. I prefer that approach. Everyone I consulted approved of my diagnosis and treatment plan."

Alison nodded, unsure of what to say next. She considered confronting Jess about the Henry VIII theory or the holes she left in her explanation of Stephen's condition, but found suddenly that she didn't want to talk about Beth anymore. It was time to change the subject, lest the anxiety tingling in her chest bloom into something more distinct.

"I'm surprised you wanted to sit with me," Alison told her.

"Why? Because we've gotten along so well?"

Alison gave her a tight smile. "Partly. Mostly because the minute I tell a lesbian that I'm bisexual, she runs in the other direction."

"Really? Why?"

Alison rolled her eyes. "Come on. You don't have to act like you don't know. It doesn't hurt my feelings anymore."

"Now I'm really confused."

"Gay girls don't like to play with bi girls. It's a thing. Everyone knows that lesbians are the most biphobic people out there."

"Ouch, that's harsh. Besides, I don't think it's true. At least not in my experience."

"Oh really? How many bi women have you dated?"

"None, but it wasn't on purpose." Alison shook her head and she protested, "It's true! I just haven't ever had the opportunity. I don't think I have, at least."

Alison's eyes slid to the volleyball court, praying the game would end. "Then you may be the only lesbian in the world who is willing to date a bi woman."

"I think that may be a bit of an exaggeration, but you seem keen on this so I'll play along. Why do we all hate you?"

"Take your pick." She ticked off the reasons on her fingers. "We don't really know whether we're straight or gay. We're greedy. We're just experimenting. Mainly, we're just stringing you along until we find a man. Every lesbian I've ever dated has been convinced that I'm going to cheat on her with a man."

The doctor looked as amused as she was thoughtful. "Because lesbians don't cheat?"

"Not with men."

"What's the difference? Is it somehow supposed to be worse if my girl cheats on me with a guy? How is it better with a woman? It's still cheating." She shifted her gaze to the table. "Still hurts like hell."

It was tantamount to a confession and surprisingly honest. After an uncomfortable moment of silence, Alison offered, "Beth tells me that you just moved here from Portland."

Jess sighed. "Yeah I did. VCU made me an offer I couldn't refuse, but I'm not sure if this is really the place for me."

"You don't like the work?"

"Oh no, I love the work." She spun her bottle between her hands, her eyes fixed on the wave of liquid sloshing around inside. "It's just that I expected things to be different."

Alison glanced over at the court, watching the arc of the ball over the net. "How so?"

Jess was quiet, and Alison looked back at her. The green eyes fixed on her were appraising. She finally said, "I hope I don't offend you here...May I call you Alison?" She waited until Alison nodded her permission. "I hope I don't offend you here, Alison, but Richmond...I mean, you guys have this whole 'rah, rah RVA' thing going, and it's cute, don't get me wrong."

"Cute?"

"Yeah. I think it's great that everyone here loves your city so much. It's just that I come from a very different place. I mean, you guys have one art museum, one gay bar, one moderately successful college sports team and you think you're, like, the up-and-coming city in America." She paused to take a sip from her bottle before continuing. "I can't tell you how many times I've heard people say 'Richmond is the next Portland.'"

"And?"

"And I just have to assume that the people who say that have never actually been to Portland. I'm sorry to tell you, this place is nothing like it. Never will be."

"Ah, yes. Because Portland is the greatest city in the world. Rome, New York, Paris, London—forget them. Portland, Oregon is the center of the universe."

Jess laughed, and there was definitely a note of self-deprecation in it. "Well Rome yeah, forget that town. It smells like sweat and garlic. New York is loud and suffers from an unfortunate excess of New Yorkers. Paris is overrated. London, on the other hand…Even Portland can't top London."

"I love London so I can't argue with that."

Jess leaned forward. "Now you see, we do have something in common."

"I don't mean to offend, but it may be the only thing."

"I suppose I deserve that. After all I did just take a shot at your hometown." She paused, color creeping up from the collar of her shirt. "I'm sorry. I'm not very good at talking to women."

Alison could feel the alcohol in her blood, and it warmed her pleasantly. "That seems unfortunate, given your career choice."

Jess laughed hard, choking on her beer. "Oh, I can talk to a woman when her feet are up in the stirrups. Then she's not a woman, she's a patient. It's just beautiful women in bars I can't seem to talk to without making a fool of myself."

Jennifer appeared at Alison's side, her sandy arm wrapped affectionately around her girlfriend's neck. "Ready to head out Ali? I need a shower and we have class first thing!"

It was astounding how oblivious Jennifer could be. She seemed to have no idea she had interrupted a conversation at such an intriguing moment. Before Alison could find words to speak, Jess excused herself and melted into the crowd. Sighing, Alison followed her friends out of the bar, her half-finished beer abandoned on the table.

CHAPTER EIGHT

"So, in our reading for last week, we were introduced to the *Querelle du Roman de la Rose*." Standing, Alison leaned against the front edge of her desk to address her class. "You'll recall this was a literary controversy that took over several European courts during the early fifteenth century. It centered on Jean de Meun's continuation of the epic poem *Romance of the Rose*. More specifically, his portrayal of women in it. Her part in the debate launched the career of Christine de Pizan. Who can tell me what her issue with de Meun was?"

Two dozen sets of eyes dipped down to their desktops. It was the standard reaction for an introductory level class. She knew that if she waited, a brave soul would rise to the challenge. That brave soul appeared in the form of an undersized boy with pouting lips and a hint of a Korean accent.

"She didn't like his language. She thought it was vulgar." He looked around to see if anyone wanted to chime in, but no one did. "She also said it was inaccurate. That a woman of high birth would never use the language he used."

"It was also how he portrayed them."

Alison turned her attention to the new speaker, an eager blonde with a long ponytail and frameless glasses. "He denigrated women. He showed all of them as sluts and gold-diggers."

"A rather modern way of putting it, but absolutely true. You're both right. By criticizing both the message and the language he used, she hit him on two fronts. Both his literary ability and his morality."

A voice piped up from the back of the room. "So she basically said 'you suck as a writer, oh and you're also a huge misogynist.'"

There was a smattering of laughter and Alison smiled. "Essentially, yes. She just used big words and a lot of sarcasm, but that's the basic idea. She used intellectualism to pick apart his work and left his supporters in the rhetorical dust. It was a formidable argument, and she caught more than a few people's eye."

Alison pushed away from the desk and paced the width of the classroom.

"Here was a woman who was standing up for women and she was eloquent and intellectual and she made this famous man look like a fool and a bully. Keep in mind this was a time of chivalry, and he was disrespectful to women."

"So, a normal man then."

More laughter for this one, and Alison turned to the girl in frameless glasses with a good-natured smile. "Oh, I've known a man or two who was nice enough. Even after the first date, if you can believe it!"

The girl in the back spoke up again and Alison recognized her as the class activist. "Didn't Simone de Beauvoir call her the first feminist?"

Alison stopped her pacing, appreciating the contribution. "She did. In 1949 she said that de Pizan demonstrated 'the first time a woman took up her pen in defense of her own sex.'"

She turned to look at the slide projected on the whiteboard behind her desk. It showed de Pizan kneeling in front of the Queen of France, presenting one of her books to the monarch. It was one of Alison's favorite depictions of de Pizan, so she always included it in her lectures. The women stood tall, their backs straight and shoulders proud, nearly identical to the portrayal of men at the time.

"We should be careful with that assessment, however. Remember that Simone de Beauvoir was a philosopher, not a historian. She was correct to say that de Pizan was unique for her time and she was certainly a strong female role model, but to call her a feminist is a bit anachronistic."

"What do you mean?" called the activist.

"I mean that de Beauvoir had a habit of bending fact to meet her own agenda. Her understanding of the time and the individual was limited." She focused on her class, hands clasped behind her back. "In any event, why don't we talk about the idea that she did defend her sex? Let's look at one of her more famous works, *The Book of the City of Ladies*. In it she discusses the virtues of a society that is built by women and which values women."

She moved back to her desk and turned to the boy with the Korean accent. "Can you tell me one of her assertions, Mr. Kim?"

He stammered a bit, and his face darkened worryingly, but he didn't have to consult his notes to answer. "She said women should recognize and embrace their ability to make peace between people."

"Absolutely correct." She gave him an encouraging smile. "Obviously she never saw women in a scrum trying to catch the bouquet at a wedding. Not much peacemaking going on there."

There was a snort from the TA's desk in the corner where Jennifer sat taking notes. More eyes were on Alison now, and they were bright with interest.

"What else?" She addressed the girl with the rimless glasses who was practically hopping in her seat. "Ms. Barnes?"

She read from her notes in a clear, carrying voice, "A woman's influence is realized when her speech accords value to chastity, virtue and restraint."

"Now you know why I don't put her in with feminism. Those aren't exactly the ideals shared by women's lib."

The activist in the back row piped up again, "Definitely not the restraint part!"

"Extra credit for a bra burning joke!"

Even Mr. Kim laughed at that. Jennifer tapped three times on her desk with the tip of her pen. It was their signal that class time was ending and Alison needed to wrap the discussion up.

"Okay. I think we'll leave it there. I don't want to go too in depth and take away all the points you're bound to make in your essays about de Pizan." The usual groan rose from the crowd at the mention of writing an essay, but Alison talked over it. "Remember folks, I'm old school. You can email me your essays or put them in my mailbox, but you will get a paper copy back with my notes. Enjoy the rest of your evening, everyone."

She stepped behind her desk while the class filed out. They were chatting among themselves, and she caught some discussion about history mixed in with the usual banter. She looked up in time to see the thin form of the women's libber squeeze past a guy with a blue mohawk to chat with Mr. Kim. The girl's smile made him blush even brighter than he had when Alison called on him, and he had to sit back down after she walked away. He stumbled out of the classroom at last, looking lost but happy.

Jennifer slid over to the front row of desks, adjusting the one his large backpack had knocked out of place. "Great discussion today."

"It was. Nice to see the class involved." Alison slumped into her desk chair, letting the stress of another day roll out of her. "There hasn't been much of that yet this semester in any of my classes."

"Well it's early yet. This group still has plenty of time to disappoint you." Jennifer laughed at her own joke. "You're not a big fan of Simone du Beauvoir, are you?"

Alison curled her lip. "Not at all. She was a rude, pedantic, sexual predator who lured impressionable teenage girls into her bed and then passed them off to Sartre as if they were her property when she was done with them. And *she's* this pioneer of feminism. Despicable."

"She was hardly the poster child for discretion, I'll give you that, but predator's a bit harsh. Her contributions to the feminist movement are undeniable. No one's perfect."

"Her least of all. I'm not a fan of moral ambiguity. That's why I'm a historian and not an ethicist."

Jennifer began to pack away her notes. "Ah, yes. The moral high ground that was the Middle Ages?"

"Precisely." Alison laughed, letting her head loll over the back of her chair and closing her eyes. "Do you think the students picked up on how much I dislike her?"

"You aren't as subtle as you like to think, Ali."

"Meaning?"

"Meaning I don't think many of them will be citing her in their essays. Well, Jerry might. He's not much on subtlety either."

"Which one is Jerry?"

"The one with the lip ring. And the nose ring. And the eyebrow ring. And the blue mohawk. Like I said, not subtle."

"Oh, right. Mr. Graves." Alison had picked up the practice of referring to her students by their last name when she studied abroad. She hadn't been able to shake the habit, so her colleagues chose to embrace it as her own little quirk. "He's also the one who doesn't know the difference between there, their and they're. Trust me, I don't expect much from him. Maybe all that metal in his face is weighing him down. Probably has misspelled tattoos too. Word is he's brilliant with numbers. I wonder if he knows Goldman Sachs has a dress code."

Jennifer dropped her bag with a bang on the desk. Alison looked up to see she was grinning from ear to ear. "Speaking of tattoos, Courtney says you were chatting up some inked hottie sporting a lesbian fauxhawk last night. I wasn't sober enough to notice, but Courtney can generally be counted on to spot the hottest chicks in any public space."

Alison sat up straighter in her chair. "Doesn't it bother you that your girlfriend checks out other women?"

"Nope." The grin on Jennifer's face gave strength to the assertion. "I know where she spends her nights."

"It doesn't make you just a touch insecure?"

"Not at all. I have abundant confidence in my sexual prowess."

"Must be nice."

"It is. So tell me about her."

Alison stood and started stuffing papers into her bag at random. "She's my friend's doctor."

"And?"

"And discussion about an idiot freshman made you think of her. That should tell you all you need to know."

"So that's it? She has tattoos and a funky hairstyle and you write her off?"

"No." She picked up her bag and headed to the door, Jennifer a step behind. "I also know she doesn't like Richmond and she is assertively happy. It's annoying."

Jennifer's laughter was drowned out by the bang of Alison shutting the classroom door behind them. "Sins beyond measure."

"I love Richmond. I grew up here. It's in my blood. The sound of the river rushing over the rapids at Pony Pasture. The view from Hollywood Cemetery. The cobblestone streets. The Greek Festival!"

"Yeah, yeah. Gyros are great and all, but seriously Prof, you need to get laid."

They reached the door to Alison's office, which she locked without going inside. "First, no one says 'Prof' anymore and second, I'm on your dissertation committee. Remember that before you insult me."

"Yeah, and you would tell me that I need more evidence than you just provided."

"I'm working on it."

"Maybe you shouldn't work so hard to find something wrong with her."

"Drop it." Jennifer slipped ahead of her and opened the stairwell door, holding it wide so Alison could walk through. "Anyway, how come your flirty girlfriend has never said *I'm* the hottest woman in the bar?"

"Who says she hasn't? I just didn't think it would do my chances at a PhD any favors if we invited my advisor to be our third."

"It definitely wouldn't." She had meant it as a joke, but she couldn't quite tell if Jennifer was joking or not. "You're sweet, but I know you're lying."

Jennifer let out an exaggerated sigh that Alison took as a sign that she was messing around. "I guess Courtney is doomed to disappointment. Anyway, I know neither of us is your type."

They pushed through the exit door and stepped out into a burst of early autumn sunshine. "Threesomes aren't my type."

"Hey, don't knock it till you try it."

"Knock. Knock. They aren't my type."

"Well, well! Alison Reynolds, full of untapped secrets!"

Alison came to a stop. "They will remain untapped, thank you very much."

Jennifer shrugged and gestured with her thumb over her shoulder. "Need an escort home?"

"No thanks." She moved off in the other direction, the ghostly silhouettes of the downtown office towers not quite visible from here, but almost. "I'm headed down to the hospital."

"Give my best to Beth. And the hot doctor."

CHAPTER NINE

Alison was still thinking about her class when she walked into the hospital lobby. She'd had precious few good discussions this school year, and she allowed herself a slice of pride over this last one. She was still thinking about it when she boarded the elevator with a small crowd, and still preoccupied when she pressed her floor button. It wasn't until a man pushed onto the elevator just before the door closed that her mind switched gears. He turned and apologized to everyone in the car, and something about his demeanor reminded her of Jess. After that her already jumpy mind wouldn't settle back on her class no matter how hard she tried to return there.

By the time the elevator doors opened and she worked her way through the crowd, her mind had drifted to her conversation with Jennifer. She wasn't really looking for a reason to dislike Jess. She didn't have to. The reasons were all right in front of her. But her mind quit its moorings once again, this time wandering to the conversation with Jess at Babe's. It hadn't been all that bad, talking to her over a beer. If she could steer the conversation away from anything she particularly cared about, there was the potential for her to end up tolerating Jess's presence after all.

Alison was so distracted that she jumped when she heard Jess's voice. She was standing halfway down the corridor, her back to Alison, deep in conversation with an older, balding man wearing brown corduroy pants with creases so straight and sharp they could have been chiseled from marble, and an ill-fitting lab coat. He faced Jess with his hands clasped behind his back, bobbing on the balls of his feet. His expression was roughly identical to the one Alison's grandfather used when she told him about what she learned in elementary school. Jess was blandly describing something that Alison assumed was about a patient, though she didn't understand much and they didn't use any names. A nurse she recognized from the previous day as Beth's hovered nearby.

The older doctor's bushy eyebrows lifted all but to what would have once been his hairline and he nodded. "That is very astute of you, Dr. Baker. I must admit, I am pleasantly surprised by your handling of this case."

"How kind of you, Dr. Emmett."

He continued as though she hadn't spoken. "I have found that physicians of your generation tend to lean toward surgical interventions rather than letting the pregnancy follow its natural course."

"Interesting. I've found that all physicians, no matter their age, follow the advice of their mentors. If the doctors here are relying too heavily on surgical intervention, perhaps we should reevaluate the way we train them. You should bring it up at the next faculty meeting."

His smile stayed perfectly in place despite the veiled insult. "A good doctor will take advice, but still blaze his own trail. No, I think age is a major factor. There is a certain arrogance to youth. It's rather pronounced in your generation, but you seem to be immune. And how old are you, Dr. Baker?"

"Old enough that your well-meaning condescension qualifies as regular old condescension, Dr. Emmett."

His veneer finally cracked. "Well! No need to be rude. I was just being polite."

"No, you were being passive aggressive, but I understand those two are the same thing here in the South."

He stared hard at her for what should have been an uncomfortably long time. She didn't so much as blink. Eventually he recognized defeat, turned on his heel and marched away. The nurse stared at Jess as though she were either some superhero brought to life or a mental patient. "Dr. Baker!"

Her voice was still stiff when she said abruptly, "Jess."

"I don't know if that was wise. Dr. Emmett has been here for longer than I've been alive. He plays golf with the governor and the attorney general."

"Sounds like he spends too damn much time on the golf course. If he spent his time here, he would find several excellent young doctors. Instead he wanders in, insults the staff and wanders off again. Maybe this place needs some new blood." Her shoulders slumped and she pinched the bridge of her nose. "I probably shouldn't have let that happen in front of you, Nancy. That was very unprofessional."

"I'm sure you can smooth it all over with Dr. Emmett."

"Oh, I don't give a shit about him. I'm apologizing to *you* for being unprofessional."

The nurse looked down and smiled at her toes. "You know he's friends with half the hospital's Medical Board right?"

"They spent too much money to bring me here to get rid of me." She smiled at the nurse, who seemed to melt a few inches into the floor. "They knew what they were getting. Too late to back out now. Anyway, I should get back to work. Was there anything else you needed, Nancy?"

She shook her head and Jess walked away, unaware of the almost slavish way Nancy's eyes followed her. Alison's jaw clenched so hard she heard her own teeth creak.

A few minutes later she burst through the door of Beth's room more forcefully than she had intended, and Beth jumped.

"Christ almighty, Alison! Are you trying to scare me into labor or what?"

"Sorry," she said, not sorry at all, and slammed her bag down. She flung herself into the chair next to the bed.

"Girl, what in the hell is wrong with you today?"

"It really bugs me when people are outright rude for no reason."

"You mean when they barge in on someone sleeping and scare them half to death?"

Alison relieved the tension in her jaw enough to stick her tongue out at Beth, but she did moderate her tone. "I mean when someone is new to an area and they refuse to adapt to the local culture."

"I'm going to go out on a limb here and assume this is about Jess?"

"Why do you say it like that?"

"Because you clearly dislike her for no reason."

"I have a reason! My reason is that she was just ridiculously rude to an older doctor. He was being a perfect Southern gentleman and she just went after him. And she did it right in front of a nurse."

Beth sat up straighter, her movement dislodging one of the many pillows behind her. Alison huffed as she stood to retrieve it. She was less than gentle when she shoved it back into place.

"And why, exactly, do you need such a ridiculous number of pillows?"

Beth crossed her hands in her lap and looked at Alison. She was silent, her face frustratingly neutral, while Alison stewed. Alison shifted and huffed again, but still Beth remained silent. She smacked the armrest of her chair with an open palm and looked around the room, determined to wait her friend out.

"Are you finished?"

"No!"

But she was. Beth had perfected that trick. Waiting patiently for the other person's mood to change. It angered stubborn witnesses and flustered opposing attorneys. Worse still, it had the most unearthly calming effect on Alison's rages.

Beth saw the change in the set of her chin and smiled. "Now, my insistence upon comfort notwithstanding, it was probably a little unprofessional of Jess to call out another doctor in front of a nurse, but why do you care so much?"

"I don't…know. It was just rude. She could learn to use a little Southern charm herself."

"Southern charm isn't about being nice to people. It's about smiling and simpering while being completely insincere. People use it as a reason to be outright rude with a smile. You throw an 'I declare' or a 'y'all' in front of it, and then you can just say any old thing you want."

"Not all Southerners are like that."

"No they aren't, but I prefer honesty. People said horrible things when we were in Boston, but at least I knew where they stood. I like my villains to own it, not dress up as decent people." She allowed herself a little grin. "The point is, not everyone handles that sort of fakeness very well. It doesn't surprise me in the least to find out that Jess is one of those people."

"I suppose you're implying that it shouldn't surprise me either?"

She grinned, showing white teeth like a wolf who scented blood. "You know, you've brought up my doctor a couple of times now. You haven't been this interested in any of them before. What's she done to get under your skin, Ali?"

The echo of Jess obliquely calling her beautiful flashed in her mind, but she wasn't ready to examine that memory. "She hasn't gotten under my skin. I just don't like her. We're like oil and water."

Beth squinted at her, but seemed content to let it rest. As she started in on discussing other things, nervousness crept into Alison. Beth wasn't the type to let something go so easily. She feared this short reprieve was only a courtroom tactic that would lead to a more intense interrogation to come.

CHAPTER TEN

By the time Alison hit her seventh red light on Broad Street she regretted driving to the hospital. It was as if the moment the sun went down all the traffic lights in the city conspired against her. She was lucky to make it more than a block or two without stopping and waiting for nonexistent opposing traffic. Around Third Street she started picturing the glass of wine she would pour herself. By the time she turned on Harrison and stopped in the middle of the road for a pack of laughing undergrads to jaywalk as slowly as humanly possible, she was contemplating skipping the glass entirely and drinking straight from the bottle.

Park Avenue, the loftily named but quiet street right off campus where Alison lived, was crowded as usual. She circled her building five times looking for a parking spot. There was nothing within a reasonable distance to her apartment. Eventually she gave up and settled on a spot several streets over, dooming herself to a considerable walk. Windows glowed orange and inviting in each house she passed. Her shoulders pinched uncomfortably at the base of her neck no matter how she adjusted her bags. Her feet screamed to be set free from their constricting shoes. At long last, she arrived at the front door of her building.

The Fan was an old neighborhood and one that Alison spent her entire youth yearning to live in. Her building had entered life as a stately row house sometime around the turn of the twentieth century. Not long before the twenty-first century the savvy owner had split it into three spacious apartments. He was an ill-mannered little troll of a man, but he'd done a fantastic job with the renovations and was always quick to respond whenever she had a concern. Rent was astronomically high, but the five-minute walk to work and the air of elegant old Richmond soaked into the bones of the place justified the expense.

Her footsteps thudded on the worn hardwood of the stairs. Each step felt like the trudge up a mountain. Not for the first time, she wished for an elevator. Her apartment was on the third floor, at the top of a creaky wooden staircase that got taller every day.

"Alison, darling, I thought that was you."

"Good evening, Mrs. Crenshaw. I'm sorry if I disturbed you."

Through the half-open door Alison could see the interior of her downstairs neighbor's apartment. Nearly every flat surface and even some not so flat ones were covered in crocheted swatches in varying shades of purple. Afghans, doilies, placemats, any and everything that could be fashioned out of yarn, Mrs. Crenshaw had made at least two. Her husband died thirty years ago, and she showed no inclination to replace him. She spent her time cooking the sort of odd things most people's grandmothers found appealing and watching game shows at increasingly eardrum-shattering volumes.

"Not at all. I was just about to sit down to an episode of *Hollywood Squares*. Care to join me?"

"Sounds tempting, but I'm afraid I have too much work tonight."

In six years Alison had never taken Mrs. Crenshaw up on an invitation, but that never seemed to bother her.

"Well, then at least take a plate of cookies with you. They've just come out of the oven."

"Oh, Mrs. Crenshaw, you don't have to…"

Alison didn't bother to finish the refusal, since her elderly neighbor was already back in the apartment, clanging about. She looked longingly up the stairs toward the sanctuary of her own front door. She wondered briefly about the likelihood of Mrs. Crenshaw following her upstairs if she bolted. Her ceramic hip wasn't likely to make the journey, but it would break her heart to be abandoned, so Alison waited.

"Here you are dear." She handed Alison a garishly decorated plate with a trio of sugared hockey pucks under plastic wrap. "Mincemeat."

A minute later, Alison dropped the plate with a clatter on her coffee table next to her keys. The light of a single table lamp was all she needed to move through the familiar confines of her apartment. Peeling her clothes off was a relief as she let each piece drop to the floor. There would be plenty of time to retrieve them in the morning. Right now, she wanted nothing more than the feel of her silk robe against her naked skin.

The bottle of wine on her kitchen counter still smelled reasonably fresh. After pouring out a glass, she saw that there was only a little more left in the bottle and it was tempting to empty the rest into her glass, but she decided against it. Tonight should be an early night. There were weeks' worth of sleep to catch up on.

She took a long sip of wine, then flopped down on the couch. Soft pillows enveloped her body. Her eyes stung, so she closed them. She nuzzled into the warm fabric, enjoying the feel of the slightly chill air on her bare legs. The knot at the base of her neck loosened ever so slightly.

If only she had someone to massage her shoulders or her feet. She had dated a massage therapist several years ago. A woman with wonderfully powerful hands but little else to recommend her. She'd kept the relationship alive for far longer than was wise just for the opportunity of an occasional foot rub. What she wouldn't give now for someone with hands like that.

Confident and sure, but with a personality to match. Someone who was intriguing without being too complicated. Funny, smart and sexy.

Unbidden, the image of Jess floated into her mind. Smiling across from her at the little wrought iron table on the back patio at Babe's. Alison sat up abruptly and reached for her wine. That was not a direction she was interested in heading. Dr. Baker was stubborn and rude. Alison had seen plain example of that today. She'd acted cocky, irreverent and childish. Not at all the kind of person Alison could or should fall for.

She swept back to the kitchen to refill her glass. The clang of the empty bottle hitting the bottom of the recycle bin made her jump. All she had in the refrigerator were a half-empty bottle of sparkling water and a stick of butter. She threw away the box of stale saltines from her pantry after only eating three. At least the wine rack wasn't empty. She rinsed her glass and dropped an ice cube into a rather too large glass of chardonnay.

Back on the couch, she found the image of Jess's half smile still firmly planted in her mind. As much as Alison hated to admit it, there was something compelling about her. All she wanted to do was lie here in the dark, drink her wine and relax, but this woman kept intruding. Alison decided it was the curve of her shoulders. They were really nice shoulders, actually. Square and strong in the way of an athlete, but still feminine. A biker or a soccer player maybe. A sport that valued toned muscles over bulging ones. The sort of physique one had to work for, but not too hard. Maybe Alison had been single too long. Maybe Beth was right about Jess getting into her head.

Beth. A bucket of ice water dropped over Alison. Her friend was hurting and here she was sitting here on her couch obsessing over an obnoxious doctor's shoulders. Meanwhile, Beth was stuck in an uncomfortable hospital bed, barely allowed to move and suffering through these draconian procedures alone. She didn't even understand why Beth was confined to a bed. How could that possibly help? How could any of this help?

"Damn!"

Digging in her purse for her phone, a dollop of wine sloshed out of her glass. Her refrigerator now would contain only butter, as the sparkling water was put to the task of cleaning her rug. She dabbed at the slowly drying spot with a dishtowel, thanking whatever luck she had remaining that she had finished the red wine before making a mess.

She took both her phone and the bottle of wine to the desk tucked into the corner of her spacious bedroom. Her computer, despite being less than a year old and the most expensive model, took an age to start up. She tapped her fingertips on the desk while she waited.

It didn't take much time scrolling through her text messages to find the one from Jess. It was the only one from an unknown number. Her thumb hovered over the hyperlink that would make her a new contact. There was little to no chance they would see each other again more than in passing. Why should she keep the number? It would only confuse her on some distant day when she scrolled through, looking for someone she actually knew. Her computer chimed its readiness. Alison touched the link and added Dr. Baker's information before she could talk herself out of it. What the hell? She had nice shoulders.

She scanned the first website for all of a minute before moving to the second. She stayed there long enough for the vein in her temple to start throbbing. Words blurred together. The tone was condescendingly gentle. Like a self-help book rather than something that might impart real information. She had to type the third address twice, misspelling it the first time when her fingers shook. Checking the address again, Alison saw Jess editorialized after entering the link.

This one is a little academic, but it's still worth reading—from a doc I studied under—one of the foremost experts in the field.

Alison snorted in disgust. Why was she shocked that a woman with more ink on her skin than in a textbook used the term "academic" as a negative? She started to read in earnest. The language was certainly more refined than the mom's blog she'd just left. After a sentence or two she opened a new browser page, clicked on the tab of her favorite websites and opened a dictionary.

She probably didn't need the dictionary. It actually wasn't that academic at all. Blood types, it explained, were based on the antigen-antibody complex. The author compared it to viruses. Like when you get the flu. The flu virus has antigens. Your body makes antibodies to fight those antigens. Once they make enough antibodies to outnumber the virus, they overwhelm and kill it.

The muffled, tinny cheering pressing up through the floor from Mrs. Crenshaw's television cut out abruptly while Alison read. Traffic noise filtering in through her bedroom windows diminished considerably. She dropped the second bottle of wine in the recycle bin and brought the plate of cookies back to her desk. The flour was stale and tasted vaguely of old yarn and dust. She chewed methodically, not bothering to work out what exactly mincemeat was. The vein in her forehead stopped throbbing.

The human body only makes antibodies if it encounters an antigen it doesn't recognize. Since Beth didn't have Kell antigens, but her son did, her antibodies were trying to kill the Kell antigens in the baby. Jess had described it before, but it made more sense now that Alison thought of the whole thing like the flu.

Apparently, Kell antibodies are very strong and particularly dangerous for pregnancies. What the author didn't spell out but Alison understood was that Beth's baby was the flu. She was, after all her miscarriages in the last two years, very good at fighting this particular type of flu. Her body would not stop until all of the invaders were gone. It was determined to kill her baby, and there was nothing she could do about it.

Alison finished the article and went back to the mom's blog. To her amazement, the information was accurate, if colloquially expressed. She brought her knees up to her chest, absentmindedly pressing the heel of her hand hard into one foot and then the other. She went back to the first page when she finished with the blog. It was somewhere between the other two, an article for a popular magazine from many years ago.

The world went silent and still while she read. When she threw herself into bed well past midnight, Alison was calm enough, or drunk enough, to fall immediately into a deep, dreamless sleep.

CHAPTER ELEVEN

"Hold the elevator!"

Alison ran through the hospital lobby to make the elevator before the doors closed. She wasn't wearing her usual sandals today, but the heeled ankle boots she had paired with her slacks weren't intended for running across waxed tile. Just when she thought she didn't have a prayer of making it in time, a hand appeared between the closing doors and they lurched to a stop.

"Ms. Reynolds."

The open doors revealed Jess. Alison stepped in and they stood awkwardly side by side. She pointedly averted her eyes from Jess's shoulders and drew her bag close as the car started to move. Jess fidgeted beside her. In the week she had been visiting this place, Alison never knew the elevators to move quite so agonizingly slowly.

Alison finally said, "You left so quickly the other night you didn't give me a chance to thank you for the drink."

"Oh, yeah. You're welcome."

"Were your friends mad at you for abandoning them?"

"Not exactly." There was a distinctly bitter edge to Jess's voice when she continued. "I'm not sure they knew I was gone. It turns out that the ex-girlfriend Adrienne was trying to hook up with was also Connie's ex-girlfriend. I missed the worst of it, but let's just say it's going to be an awkward few days down in the pharmacy."

"They aren't together? Your friends?"

"Oh, no. Both butches. Both very butch butches. I'm actually kind of surprised they don't have more old flames in common, but then we've only hung out a few times. Maybe the fireworks are normal and I just haven't been around to see them."

"They probably do have a lot of exes in common. If you've been to Babe's twice then you've met every lesbian in Richmond. We keep a tight pack."

"I kinda picked up on that." She tapped a fingernail against the railing behind her. "Do you run into a lot of exes there?"

"Not many. The ladies don't like my kind remember?"

Jess scratched behind her ear. "You said that. I thought it was your subtle way of telling me to leave you alone."

Alison smiled, thinking about Jennifer's recent assessment of her. "I'm told I'm not overly subtle."

Jess gave her a quizzical look, but shifted quickly to the pleasant neutral of her doctor demeanor. "Did you have a chance to look at those articles I sent you?"

"I did." Despite the pounding headache she woke up with, her reading last night had actually made Alison feel better. The more she understood Beth's situation, the more comfortable she felt with the process. "I meant to thank you."

"Don't mention it. I'm just glad they helped."

"Not as much as a few beers and some dancing." She looked at her toes as the interminable elevator ride finally ground to a halt. "But it's nice to understand a little better."

"I'm happy to provide both beer and knowledge, but it's a good thing you found another source for the dancing."

Jess held the door, but Alison waited to walk beside her. "You don't dance?"

"I have a few strengths, but rhythm is not one of them."

"Anyone can dance. All you have to do is move with the music."

"You say that like it's so easy."

"It is. You just let go and follow your body."

"My body hasn't made wise decisions on the dance floor in the past."

"Maybe you just haven't had the right partner."

"Maybe."

When the charming half smile appeared on Jess's lips, Alison switched to a safer topic. "How's Beth?"

"Stir-crazy already. That doesn't bode well for the next few weeks." They turned a corner, heading toward Antepartum and slowed their pace as they talked. "But she's probably the best patient we have. A lot of women get nervous about being pregnant. Throw in a high-risk situation and it's a recipe for short tempers. Beth hasn't snapped once. The nurses love her. Nancy in particular is very fond of her."

"Beth isn't the only one she's fond of."

The words were out of her mouth before she realized she was thinking them. Jess turned to her. "What do you mean?"

"I just meant…" She smiled to cover her embarrassment. "The staff here seems to like you very much. I get the impression they aren't overly fond of some of the older doctors."

"No, they aren't." Jess's mouth tightened. "Some doctors don't treat nurses well. I read an article once that said eighty percent of nurses have been yelled at by a doctor at least once in their career."

"That has to be an exaggeration."

"I wish it were. The real number is probably higher. Some nurses see bad treatment as part of the job." Alison had to pick up her pace to keep up with Jess. "We're under enormous stress as physicians, but that doesn't give us the right to treat anyone poorly. Combine stress with the demographics of the two professions, and it leads to an inevitable result."

"You mean that most doctors are men and most nurses are women?"

"Partly, but not all men are rude and not all women are meek. I mean that most doctors are from money and privilege.

We tend to be type A personalities. People who are spoiled and used to getting their way."

"Does that describe you?"

Jess shrugged. "My family certainly didn't struggle when I was growing up, but we were blue collar."

"I'm sorry. That was overly personal. I don't know what's gotten into me today."

"Not at all! I'm proud of my parents' work ethic." She smiled at Alison. "I am a little spoiled though. You may have noticed that in my lack of enthusiasm about Richmond."

"Lack of enthusiasm is rather mild."

"I guess I'm just as loyal to my hometown as you are to yours." She shrugged again, and her smile lent the gesture a flippancy that Alison appreciated. "Anyway, there was this nurse when I was coming up. She was one of the first medical professionals who accepted me as a doctor, and she always made a point of reminding me that we're a team in hospitals. We depend on each other. None of us can do the other's job. We're equally important to the process of healing, even if some of us get reserved parking spaces. I took that with me."

"She sounds like a very special person."

They reached the nurses station, and Jess stopped. "She was. She still is. She's retired now, but she never misses an opportunity to lecture me."

Alison was intrigued. She pictured the weathered old face of her own mentor. Her advisor when she was in Boston who had taught her so much that she always left his office feeling as if she was carrying the weight of a library in her mind. She hadn't spoken to him in over a year, not since attending a conference in Boston, but she could still remember the exact inflection he used when he said her name.

"You still talk to her? Even though you've moved across the country?"

"Well, she gets very upset if I don't check in." Jess leaned forward and whispered, "She's my mother. Don't tell anyone here. It would ruin my rebel without a cause reputation if they found out I call home twice a week."

Alison smiled. Jess's buoyant nature was infectious.

"Well if you'll excuse me, Ms. Reynolds…Alison. I should be going."

"Thank you for holding the elevator, Dr. Baker…Jess."

Forgetting her determination not to admire Jess's shoulders, Alison watched her disappear down the hall into the bowels of the hospital before continuing on her own way. She strolled toward Beth's room, tracing the path that was fast becoming familiar with the happy anticipation that always came with a few uninterrupted hours of gossip with her best friend.

CHAPTER TWELVE

Alison found fall in Richmond equal parts exhilarating and infuriating. Being both in the South and within barking distance of the ocean made the weather unpredictable. She'd endured Septembers that were as hot as the middle of summer, and some when a cold snap rushed in bringing that fresh chill of autumn before anyone could reasonably expect it. So when one of those cold snaps hit the next day, Alison walked out of her last class, holding the strap of her leather briefcase tight to her chest, wishing she'd had more sense than to wear this thin sweater. Wishing it could somehow thicken into something more substantial by sheer force of will.

As she opened the glass doors of the Hibbs Building and stepped out into the evening, a hint of sunlight fell on her shoulder and tried valiantly to warm her. Jennifer followed her through the door, continuing to discuss their last class.

"I would expect this kind of laziness from freshmen, but this is a four hundred level class. They're history majors. They can't possibly think that discussion was what you expect."

Less than two months into the semester, her students were uninterested and lazy. One good discussion about Christine de Pizan aside, not one of her classes was fully engaged. Alison was a notoriously tough grader, and she worried that this class would fare even worse than her usual low standard. Unfortunately, she also knew it was entirely her fault. A classroom took its cues from the professor, and she was not focused on her classes. Good professors knew that a bad grade was as much their failure as the student's. She had failed to inspire, failed to kindle that thirst for knowledge that had brought them into her classroom to start with. Alison was failing this class and she needed to shake herself out of her funk or risk losing them entirely.

Jennifer wasn't exactly perceptive of her mood. While she railed on about the inadequacies of their students, Alison scanned the courtyard, hoping none of them were present to hear. Fortunately, it was early evening and most traffic was heading to the dining hall across the courtyard. There was, however, a familiar face nearby.

Jess leaned casually against a concrete half-wall a few feet away wearing a black hoodie and a mildly bored expression. She watched the swarms of undergrads around her, her hands buried in her pockets. Alison was used to feeling a flare of annoyance when she saw Jess, but today she had to admit that interest had replaced it. She couldn't quite pinpoint when things had shifted, but apparently Beth was right, Jess had gotten under her skin. She just hadn't expected that to be a good thing.

"Ali? Earth to Ali? Can you hear me?"

Jess spotted her. The boredom disappeared in an instant, replaced by a glowing smile. Alison's stomach squirmed pleasantly as she smiled back.

"Isn't that the woman you were talking to at Babe's the other night? The one Courtney thought was so hot? My girl has good taste."

She nodded in response to Jennifer's question, then instantly forgot her existence, barely registering the knowing chuckle and retreating footsteps as she moved across the brick pavers toward the half-wall.

"Nice to see you again, Dr. Baker. What brings you to my side of campus tonight?"

Jess's smile widened as Alison leaned against the cold stone. "Just as stubborn as your BFF, aren't you?"

Jess waited, smiling but silent, until the penny finally dropped. "Sorry, nice to see you again *Jess*."

"Much better. I was nearby and thought I might convince you to get a cup of coffee with me. I hear Lamplighter is good and it's just around the corner."

A warmth that was far more effective than the weak sunlight spread through Alison. "Are you asking me on a date?"

Color glowed across Jess's smooth cheeks making her look years younger. "I'm from Portland remember? Coffee is a religion for us. Well, beer too, but it's a little early for drinking."

She trailed off, looking around at the crowd. After Jess had challenged her on the name, Alison wasn't going to let her off so easy. "You didn't answer my question."

Jess laughed throatily and dug her hands deeper into her pockets. "I thought my adorable awkwardness would be answer enough."

"It isn't."

Jess rubbed her neck, her smile creating an irresistible twinkle in her eye. "Okay. You win. Yes, I'm asking you on a date." Her hand stilled on her neck. She had rubbed it pink. "Are you accepting?"

"Of course."

* * *

Alison suggested they sit outside. Lamplighter Roasting Company was a coffee shop wedged into a repurposed auto shop, complete with plexiglass garage doors and artfully stained concrete floors. The back patio was fenced in and surrounded by trees whose limbs were wrapped in white Christmas lights, making it a beautiful spot for a first date. Dusk settled around them, the lights twinkled like fairies. They sat in a secluded corner, the smell of roasting beans and steaming milk reaching them even out here.

As soon as they sat down with steaming lattes in front of them, Jess asked, "So you teach history right? What's your specialty?"

Alison gripped the ceramic mug, trying to draw warmth from it. She had suggested the choice of table, but now the chill of nervousness had replaced the warm flush of anticipation. "Medieval European. I specialize in the history of women during the Late Middle Ages."

Jess sipped her coffee, pondering. "Fascinating time period. There's a lot to cover there."

Alison was used to this type of vague reply. People rarely knew much about history, particularly the Middle Ages, but no one liked to admit it. Most people were intimidated by her intelligence, and often hostile to it. So many evenings had ended embarrassingly early when a date pretended to know more than they did, or told her she was wasting her time with a worthless subject. Occasionally, they would try to cover their ignorance by asking leading questions, hoping to sound knowledgeable when they really weren't. It didn't bother her if they didn't know anything about her work, it was the subterfuge that bothered her. She was disappointed but not really surprised that Jess was one of the leading question types.

"It is fascinating, isn't it? What are your favorite subjects in the Late Middle Ages?"

Jess set her coffee cup down, looking into the distance. "I'll admit I'm no expert. Wasn't the Avignon Papacy during the late Middle Ages? The little squabbles between popes are always fun. Or was that the High Middle Ages? It all kind of runs together for me when the church is involved. Then there's the Hundred Years War and the Spanish Inquisition. Torture and battles. I'm partial to the Black Death." She smiled at the way Alison's eyebrow arched. "For obvious reasons."

Alison shivered hard enough to nearly lose control of her voice. "Obvious reasons?"

Jess unzipped her hoodie and stood, walking around the table and dropping it over Alison's trembling shoulders. She leaned down, the warmth of her body remarkably close, and said, "I'm a doctor after all."

The cotton of the hoodie was soft and warm, with a light but musky perfume and the slightest hint of some citrus scent that made her eyebrow stay arched. "Of course."

Jess laughed her throaty laugh, dropping back into her chair. She was wearing a thick, long sleeve knit shirt with a V-neck in a warm blue that set off her eyes in what she had to know was a devastating way. "You thought I wouldn't know anything about medieval history."

Alison slid her arms through the sleeves of the hoodie. It was maybe a size too big, but not too bulky. "Most people don't." She looked up at Jess meaningfully through her eyelashes. "Thank you, by the way. I should have worn a jacket."

Jess sat rigidly for a moment and then waved her hand dismissively. She took a sip of coffee that was too large to be advisable, but managed not to choke on it.

Alison had been on a lot of dates recently, most of them dreadful. Beth kept telling her that she had to kiss a lot of frogs to find a princess and even more to find a prince, but the pool of interesting partners seemed to be dwindling. Dating in your thirties was supposed to be fun, but she found it depressing.

She'd joined an online dating service, but it was a lot of work sifting through the possibilities and that work never seemed to pay off. She pretended to pay only passing interest in the site but actually checked several times a day. After a string of awful dates she would shut it down, determined to let love find her. Then a few lonely weeks would go by and she would reactivate it, only to be disappointed again. The whole thing just made her feel empty. Overall, it had been a very long time since she had sat across from a stranger and felt like this. Like she already knew she wanted a second date.

As she pondered the upswing in her dating prospects, they chatted easily about history. Jess was not only somewhat knowledgeable on the subject, but, more importantly, interested to learn more. She made a hobby of taking open online courses on a wide range of topics from history to literature to science. The phenomenon of online courses for no credit was new to Alison, and Jess lit up at the chance to explain the pleasures of being an itinerant student. Time slipped past at a dizzying rate.

When Jess asked if she'd like a refill she gladly accepted. She sat alone at the table, grinning up at the first stars poking through the city lights while Jess went inside to get their new cups.

"You a *Mass Effect* fan?"

Alison shifted her eyes from the sky to a see a man in his early twenties leaning on the back of the vacant chair.

"Beg pardon?"

He pointed a stubby finger at her chest. "*Mass Effect.*"

She just blinked in reply.

"Your hoodie. I just figured."

She looked down in confusion at the black cotton. The logo on the chest was a white 'N7' with a red triangle situated right below one shoulder. A red stripe ran down the shoulder from collar to cuff, bracketed by a thinner white stripe on both sides. She hadn't noticed the hoodie's logo before, only the woman inside it.

"Sorry, it's not mine."

"It's mine actually." Jess came up behind him, setting their coffees on the table. "She was cold."

"Oh. Cool."

He looked like he was going to slink off, but Jess stopped him. "I'm a bit obsessed with *Mass Effect*, to be honest. All three games. The first one's a little cheesy and the graphics are terrible compared to what you can get these days, but it's still awesome."

His grin came back and he shifted his full attention to Jess. "Totally. Do you Fem Shep?"

"Come on man, look at me! Of course! Give me a chance to play a badass soldier who saves the galaxy three times and you let me make her a woman if I want to? I've never once picked the guy."

"That's cool. I started out as the guy, but the voice acting for Fem Shep is too good. I played her once and was hooked. Now I'm Fem Shep all the way."

"Very progressive of you. Way to go man. Are you Renegade or Paragon?"

"Renegade! I dig the scars. Plus it's fun to say all the evil stuff you never would in real life. You?"

"Paragon." After sliding Alison's coffee to her with a wink, she continued, "I'm old fashioned. I like my heroes to be all nice and, well, heroic."

They laughed together. Alison had no idea what they were talking about, but the whole thing was rather charming. She guessed the kid didn't talk to women much. He seemed to be close to hyperventilating just having a conversation of this length.

Jess's tone turned serious. "Who do you romance?"

"Liara of course! You?"

"Definitely Liara. Every time. True blue, all the way through."

"Have you seen the trailer for the new one?"

"Oh, yeah. I can't wait for it to come out. I check for the release date announcement every day."

"Me too!"

"I'm sure they'll hate me at work for this, but I'm taking off at least a couple days to marathon play when it comes out."

He held out his hand and they fist bumped. "Cool." He shot a look at Alison, but she was sure this time he was checking out the hoodie instead of her. "I'll let you get back to your coffee."

Jess gave him a wave and dropped into her chair. She didn't seem like she was going to offer an explanation, so Alison asked, "What was that about?"

"The hoodie is from a game series I play." She sipped her coffee before continuing. "So I should probably tell you at this point that I'm a gamer. Another hobby. Or probably more accurately called an obsession."

"What do you mean? You mean, like, you play video games?" Jess nodded and she continued, "Oh. That's...surprising."

"Why is that surprising?"

"I just thought you would be interested in things more... doctor-like."

"Oh, yeah? Like I should sit at home every night in my smoking jacket with a pipe and a monocle, reading *Gray's Anatomy* for fun?"

Alison's cheeks were suddenly warm in the chill air. "Not exactly. But video games? I mean…"

Jess sat forward, her grin still good-natured, but slipping a fraction. "Please don't say 'aren't you a little too old for that.' You'll sound like my mom."

Alison shrugged, pretending she wasn't about to say exactly that.

"I'm not the only one. Most gamers are older these days. We're from the generation that made video games popular. We were raised on them, so it's natural for us to still like them when we get older. It's way more interactive than watching TV. It engages my mind and at the same time lets me relax. Why is that so bad?"

"I didn't say it was bad, it's just…It just seems kind of juvenile. Aren't video games violent and disrespectful to women? You know, guys living in their parents' basements with no job, playing online all day and night, calling their friends slurs and being all around unpleasant."

"That's the stereotype, and you must know by now I don't buy stereotypes. Some games are violent and some are disrespectful to women, but no more than most of the summer blockbuster movies. A lot of games are very inclusive and not at all sexist. In *Mass Effect* you can choose to play with either a male or a female hero. Either character can date both male and female characters."

"What do you get out of it, though?"

"I like games with a good story. When you find a great game and win, it's an amazing feeling. Sort of like finishing a good book, only you have a part in telling the story. But now I'll really blow your mind. Gaming makes me a better doctor."

The original argument intrigued Alison, but this last was too much. She scoffed.

"You don't believe me?"

"No, sorry, I don't buy it. How does playing video games make you a better doctor?"

Jess grinned, her smile crooked, revealing just a few bright white teeth on one side. Alison's stomach fluttered again. The playful light in Jess's eyes was bewitching. The rest of the patio seemed miles away.

"Puzzles. It's all about puzzles."

"What do you mean?"

"A really challenging role-playing game isn't that different from a medical case. You have an objective in a game, say sneaking into a building. You try a first-floor window but it's locked, so you climb to the second-floor balcony and try the door. Once you get inside you're faced with a completely new set of problems. Bad guys patrolling the top floor. Figure out their sentry pattern so you can move from one room to the next unseen."

Jess talked with her hands, her fingers dancing along the surface of the table as though she were drawing a floorplan. The hairs on Alison's arm stood up as she got another wave of the scent on Jess's jacket.

"It's not that different from figuring out what's wrong with a pregnancy. You have to keep your mind open. Consider all the different possibilities based on the symptoms and then rule them out, one by one. You try something. It doesn't work, so you try something else. All the while the lives of a woman and her baby are on the line and you are the only one who can save them." Her hands stopped moving and she looked into her half-full coffee cup. "Is it so shocking that I would want to have that feeling of accomplishment over a princess in a castle instead of a patient in pain? No one dies. The good guy always wins. Unlimited do-overs. I always get the girl. Happily ever after. And usually with a killer soundtrack."

Alison looked up, staring into those jade-green eyes until she realized Jess was waiting for her to say something. She hadn't realized how long she had been quiet. While she'd been watching Jess, her feet had been swept out from underneath her. Then those eyes picked her up and swept her away.

Her mind fluttered around, trying to find something to talk about. She should be good at this, with all the first dates she had been on, but her thoughts were moving too slowly tonight. She finally blurted out, "So…are you from Portland originally?"

"Born and raised."

"I thought no one was really from Portland. Didn't the whole population just move there to be cool?"

"Almost everyone," she replied with a laugh. "My parents bought a dirt-cheap little rancher near Cathedral Park right after they got married. They're real Portland. Granola types. We were composting back before people did that for show. My dad rode a bicycle to work before they had bike lanes."

"Sounds nice."

"Are you kidding? That was the eighties! Conspicuous consumption and processed foods. Eating organic peanut butter you had to stir the oil back into was not cool. I had to sneak into arcades for years before they would buy me a Nintendo, and it was right before the Super Nintendo came out so it wasn't cool anymore. I wanted neon blue sunglasses and tie-dye shirts. I got shit made out of hemp. I hated it."

Alison snorted into her coffee then held her mouth closed with cold fingers to keep her giggles in. They laughed and talked until their table was full of empty mugs and the barista turned off the lights out front.

CHAPTER THIRTEEN

Three days after her coffee date, Alison walked toward Beth's hospital room with more weight in her step than usual. She surveyed all the halls, but without any real hope of seeing Jess. It seemed she was doomed to disappointment where her new crush was involved. Despite assurances that they would meet again soon, Jess had not called since they left Lamplighter. Every day Alison came to visit Beth, every day she lingered in hopes of seeing her, and every day she left a little more deflated.

Beth sat up in her nest of pillows, face creased in concentration. Files were stacked on the table in front of her, pushed out a little farther than normal because of her swollen belly.

"I'm pretty sure you're not supposed to be working while you're on bed rest."

Beth flinched as her concentration broke. "Probably not, but I have cases pending and I'm going crazy sitting here doing nothing."

Alison pulled a chair over to the bed, peeking at the case files as she sat. "You haven't been doing nothing. You had another transfusion today."

"I don't do anything during those, just lay still and try not to freak out." Beth snapped the file shut. A shudder ran through her and her dark complexion paled a shade. "And stop trying to look at my case files! You're just as bad as Stephen. He's always snooping when I work at home."

"You try all of the juicy cases. Of course we want to sneak a peek!"

"No murderers or corrupt congressmen in this batch. Just some pro bono work to help out the public defender's office."

"Doing your part to save the world?"

Her voice hardened as she replied, "Always."

She adopted the expression Alison called her "crusader face." Beth had grown up the daughter of hard-working, white-collar African-American parents who knew the uniqueness of their success. They struggled to earn a better life for themselves and their children amid the most unforgiving of circumstances. They lost their first child, a son, before they had Beth and never fully healed from the grief. It made them appreciate all the more what they had. They gave their only daughter every advantage in education and opportunity, but never allowed her to forget that they were the lucky ones.

Beth was an excellent, and thus expensive, criminal defense attorney; but she spent a good deal of her time defending the poor and marginalized of the Richmond community. Her firm allowed her the time because they knew she had her pick of jobs elsewhere if they pushed her too far. Some people, both white and black, resented her for her success and her charity, but she was stubborn enough to ignore her critics. The people she helped needed her more she needed universal popularity.

Alison cleared her throat. "Speaking of Stephen, what's with the ponytail?"

Beth's whole aspect changed, as it often did when she spoke about her husband. She smiled wickedly and leaned toward Alison. "It's hot, right? I just wanna grab him by that ponytail and ride him like a cowboy."

"Um…eww."

Beth laughed, falling back into her pillows. "Sorry Ali. You know how I get when I'm pregnant."

"Beth, you're horny as a teenager *all* the time!"

"True, but only with him." She paused, raising one perfectly plucked eyebrow. "Speaking of…"

"What?"

"You and my doctor."

The heat on Alison's face was like a furnace. "I don't know what you're talking about."

"You know that I've met you, right? You show up here every day like an excited puppy, and when she's not around you pout. A week ago you were ready to run her out of town, and now you're practically drooling all over her!"

"That's not…I…" She looked away. "So she won me over with how well she's cared for you. I do have an open mind you know."

Beth pursed her lips and crossed her arms, tapping one long fingernail against her forearm.

The battle was lost and all she could do was try to salvage a fraction of dignity. "Okay. We bumped into each other at Babe's."

Beth's voice was a suggestive purr. "I knew it! Bumped into her? How many times? Was there screaming? I want details!"

"Stop it! We had one beer. Well, we also had coffee the other day. That's all."

"That's *not* all."

"Yes, it is. She hasn't called since." She slumped back in her chair. "She's not that into me. Gay girls never are. Besides, she's not my type."

"You're a terrible liar. She's totally your type. That sort of confident swagger and the baby face. Not too butch, not too femme. What do your people call that?"

"My people? You're so annoying." She smiled, though, and answered, "Androgynous. Just andro really, or genderqueer, but I'm too old to use that term. Anyway, that's not the point. Did you miss the part about how gay girls aren't into me? How she hasn't called me since?"

Beth waved the denials away, flipping her wrist so dismissively that Alison's temper flared. "She's spent the last two days on ER duty. I didn't even see her. More importantly, Ali, you need to get over this conviction that all lesbians hate bisexuals."

"They do!" Alison heard how loud she was and tempered her tone before continuing, "They do. You know what I've been through."

"You have one girlfriend, one asshole girlfriend, blame leaving you on the fact that you're bisexual, and now you think the whole community is full of bigots." She pointed an accusatory finger at Alison. "I told you from the start she wasn't good enough for you, but you ignored me. One jerk doesn't make a rule. You're just looking for a reason and you know it."

"I don't need a reason. I haven't had a single lesbian go on more than a few dates with me since. They just aren't into me."

Beth's eyebrow arched again and she said, "Well, *she's* into you. Or she wants to be in…"

"Stop it!" Alison looked around even though she knew they were alone. She hissed, "Stop right there! You are riddled with hormones. What if someone hears you?"

"You're no fun!"

They looked at each other for a long moment, and then fell into laughter. It was just like the old days when they shared an apartment and stayed up all night watching chick movies and drinking endless bottles of cheap wine. Lost in the happiness, neither noticed the sound of a cane clicking behind them on the tile floor.

"Surprise, surprise. The partners in crime."

Beth lit up. "Momma! Daddy!"

At the sight of Beth's parents Alison smiled almost as broadly as Beth. They were the picture of graceful aging. Now closing in on their mid-seventies, lines carved their faces like old tree trunks. But there were more laugh lines than worry lines, and the healthy silver of their hair was proof of a life well lived. Beth's father walked with a cane since having his knees replaced a few years earlier, and her mother's hand wrapped around his free arm. Both had skin much darker than Beth's, with her mother's a shade darker than her dad.

"The two terrors are at it again, I see." Her mother's voice was low and rolling like thunder across a Midwestern plain, and carried a musical quality Beth had inherited. "Good evening, Alison dear. How are you?"

Alison moved to the pair, kissing both lightly on the cheek. "I'm well Mama J. How are you?"

Beth's father answered, "She's surly and unmanageable. Same as she's been for fifty-one years."

The joke was an old one, and his wife rolled her eyes in response. Still, her hand gripped ever so lightly on his arm. It was an affectionate gesture, born of the kind of love and respect that only two people who have spent their entire lives in each other's company could share. She watched as those bent hands and swollen knuckles flexed around the only arm Beth's mom had ever held, and her heart ached.

"How's our daughter?"

"Just as surly and unmanageable." She looked over at Beth, who stuck out her tongue.

"And your parents?"

"On another cruise."

"The benefits of living in Tampa. Where are they going this time?"

"I'm not sure." Alison pulled the strap of her purse higher on her shoulder. "When I called they were heading for port. It was a last-minute deal. Mom forgot to email me their itinerary."

Lines cut deeper into her face as Beth's mother pursed her lips. "And your sisters?"

Alison hadn't spoken to either of them in several weeks. "They're fine. Busy."

"Send our love to all when you speak to them next."

"Of course. I'll leave this one to you." She jerked her thumb at Beth, who was packing away her files. "Try to get her to rest."

"Not much chance of that." Beth's father smiled at her. "Take care, dear."

"Yes, sir. Of course."

She gave Beth a little wave and stepped out into the hall. She scanned the nurses station and the hall with a sigh. The sigh cut off abruptly when she saw Jess standing in the little alcove where they had talked the day they met. She was wearing scrubs today, light blue and a little baggy with a cap tied around her hair. Alison's stomach flipped the same way it had on their date. She squared her shoulders and started toward the alcove.

Jess's face was fixated on the screen of her phone as though her life depended on it. She tapped the screen hard with her thumb and put the phone to her ear, shaking tension from her shoulders and blowing out a deep breath. She stood, shifting her weight from one foot to the other, waiting for her call to connect. Alison was just a few steps away when her purse began to ring. Jess turned to the noise and nearly jumped out of her skin.

"Alison! I was just…"

She snatched the ringing phone from the depths of her purse.

"I was just calling you."

Alison smiled, turning her phone to show Jess her own name on the display. "I noticed."

Jess kept the phone to her ear as she spoke. "I'm sorry I haven't called. I wanted to, but the ER here has been crazy busy. I don't know what happened in this town nine months ago, but there were an awful lot of busy couples out there and they all showed up fully dilated this weekend." She looked around the hall. "I was on ER rotation this weekend, did I mention that? All the docs in the hospital have to rotate to the ER once a month."

Alison smiled and said in a soft voice, "You can hang up the phone, you know."

Jess looked at the phone in her hand as though she had never seen it before. Then she tapped the screen with her thumb and dropped it into the pocket of her scrubs. "Right. Like I was saying…What was I saying?"

"You weren't lying. You are definitely not good at talking to women."

Jess rubbed at the fabric of the cap tied around her hair. It was decorated with little pixelated white and green mushrooms with smiling cartoon faces. "No. I wasn't lying at all."

Alison reached out, touching Jess's arm. Just the slightest brush of her fingertips along her forearm, but Alison could feel the tight bands of muscle under the warmth of her skin. She pushed back the desire to run her fingers down to Jess's hand, grab it tight and hold on. "You were saying that you meant to call me."

Jess stared at the spot where her fingers touched. "Right. Yes!" She grinned, getting a firmer grip on the situation. "I meant to call you, but I didn't and I'm really sorry. I was hoping I could make it up to you."

"And how did you plan to do that?"

Jess could tell she was going to say yes and it made her bolder. She took a step forward, closing the gap between them from friendly to something more intimate. "I'd like to take you to dinner. There's a French place in Shockoe Bottom I hear good things about. Are you free tomorrow night?"

"It just so happens that I am."

CHAPTER FOURTEEN

"Tell me about your family."

Alison spun her fork between her fingers. "My parents live in Florida. I have two older sisters. Both of them live out West."

"What do they do?"

"As little as possible."

Jess laughed into her napkin and Alison took a bite of her excellent boeuf bourguignon. Bistro Bobette rode the line between fine dining and bistro perfectly, helped by an extremely talented chef who had mastered that uniquely French ability to make food both simple and wonderfully complex in the same bite. It was evident in the rich base of her stew and also in the light and acidic lemon butter sauce on Jess's fish.

Their table sat in a corner formed by an exposed brick wall and the wide glass windows fronting the street. Café curtains gave them privacy, but also allowed them to snoop on the thick crowds on the sidewalk. Shockoe Bottom was a popular nightspot, boasting the best restaurants in the city and the loudest bars. Bistro Bobette was at the top of the district, just a block from the spot where high-rise office buildings gave way to restaurants but still several blocks from the beginning of the nightclubs. It was crowded, but it was a calm sort of crowded.

They spent the first few awkward moments looking out through the windows. It didn't take long for them to focus in on each other, and soon the world buzzed around them without any notice. The other tables filled, emptied and filled again as they chatted and ate.

Jess asked, "So you got all of the ambition in the family?"

"I don't know if you'd call it ambition. I just like what I do." The waiter cleared away their empty plates and Alison leaned her elbows on the white tablecloth. "My sisters take after my parents. Mom and Dad both came from old money and spent their working lives doing just enough to keep from losing their status. These days we don't talk much."

The waiter placed cups of coffee in front of them along with a towering slice of chocolate mille crepe cake and two forks.

"Did something happen between you?"

"No. We just aren't the sort." Alison's fork slid through the cake, dark chocolate oozing luxuriously from between the layers. "They retired to Florida the minute my dad could start drawing a pension."

"How very stereotypical of them. Don't they have phones in Florida?"

Alison laughed into her coffee cup. Steam billowed into her eyes. "They do, but my family's never been the two phone calls a week kind of people."

Jess's forkful of cake hovered in front of her mouth. "You are. You come to see Beth almost every day."

For the first time all night, Alison begrudged the empty wineglass in front of her. Jess was on call, so drinking wasn't an option. She had tried to convince Alison to order a glass, but it seemed like a chance to see how things would go without alcohol. She had to admit it was nice; but talking about her family was always easier with wine.

"Beth's more than family. Especially more than my family."

The waiter arrived with the check and Alison reached for her purse. Jess handed him her credit card without looking inside the folder.

"What are you doing?"

"I'm not the kind of person who splits the check on a date."

Alison bristled. "And if I am that kind of person?"

"Then I sincerely hope this is the one and only way I disappoint you." She nodded to the waiter and he left, smiling, with the card. "But I will have to disappoint you."

Jess pushed the remaining cake toward her. Eating the last bite felt like adequate revenge. "I suppose I can look at it as old-fashioned rather than condescending."

Jess's eyes were all smoke and charm as she replied in a low voice, "Thank you for indulging me."

They lingered over coffee long enough for the staff to congregate at the bar. When they stepped out into the night, the warm ambience seemed to follow them. Alison's long skirt caught in the breeze and flapped behind her but the sound was lost in her laughter. Her scoop neck shirt pulled tight against her skin and she used the cold as an excuse to move closer to Jess. Their hands touched and Jess twined their fingers together. Warmth coursed through Alison starting at the spot their skin touched. Their eyes met for a moment, but veered away just as quickly.

They turned the busy corner past the Tobacco Company Restaurant, heading toward the garage where they both parked. Alison was as happy as if she had drunk a whole bottle of wine herself but thankfully sober enough to enjoy every moment. Her head buzzed with the sound of Jess's voice. Her eyes wandered to the slope of Jess's shoulder next to hers. She decided she'd been right all along. There was definitely something in the set of them that refused to be ignored.

Jess was finishing the story that had kept them laughing all the way down the street. "So here I am, delivering this baby in a packed ER. Mom's screaming, dad's fainted and I'm in up to my elbows, trying to get this baby out."

"Wait, the father fainted?"

Jess let go of her hand to make a motion like an umpire calling a runner safe. Alison slid her hand up Jess's arm and held just above her elbow.

"Fainted. Clean out on the floor. It happens all the time in movies, but never in real life. My nurse had to go help him, leaving me basically alone for the delivery. He nearly pulled his wife's IV out on his way down. But the best part was that, right about this time, an ambulance shows up.

"The ER there was this whole open concept thing. One massive circular room with the nurses station in the center and all the rooms around it like a clock with a room at every hour mark. They wheel in this elderly patient who'd decided to do a little self-medicating for her arthritis."

"Self-medicating?"

"Jack Daniels. The whole bottle by the smell of her. She's screaming at the top of her lungs. Cussing like a sailor and fighting the EMTs. I'm delivering this baby at three o'clock and they wheel her into four o'clock. We could hear every filthy name she called the staff."

Alison giggled and leaned against Jess's arm.

"So I got the baby out. Perfect little boy. Easy delivery in the end. I left the room just as the arthritis patient slipped out of her restraints. They got her in a gown, but she tore it off as she ran down the hall. She's still wearing her fuzzy slippers and now the only other thing she's got on is a pair of underpants that look like she got them during the Eisenhower administration."

"You're so making this up!"

"I am not. I swear! All of this totally happened."

Alison leaned against Jess, gripping her arm and pressing their hips together. Jess looked at the hand wrapped around her arm and her smile slipped a little.

"Um…anyway. Right. Drunk old lady. She barrels me over and I hold on for dear life, knowing there'll be a nurse tech along any minute to help. So there I am, rolling around on the floor trying to hold on to a half-naked woman twice my age fighting me like she's possessed. She landed a nasty right hook smack on my jaw before they finally get a sedative into her. And let me tell you, that thing about seeing stars? Absolutely real."

"She punched you?"

They had reached Alison's car.

"My jaw still clicks." Jess gave the vehicle a sour look. "Then she said the 'tattooed biker chick' tried to assault her. Made up this whole story. Said I grabbed her and threw her to the ground and nearly broke her hip. Wanted to sue the hospital. Once she was sober, they showed her surveillance video of her antics and she went away quietly. Sent me a lovely apology letter. On pink stationery with her name embossed at the top no less."

Alison took a hesitant step toward her car, pulling the keys from her purse as slowly as she could. "Does that happen a lot? Patients acting like that about the way you look?"

Jess shrugged, pushing her hands deep into her pockets. "You mean like you did?" She winked. "All the time. They leave me alone when I start to treat them and they find out I know what I'm doing. I've learned to ignore it."

"Why, though?"

"Why what?"

"Why learn to ignore it? Why keep it all? The hair and the tattoos and all. Doesn't it make it harder to get people to respect you as a doctor? Why not...I don't know..."

"Change?"

"Yeah...maybe."

"I'm a square peg, Ali." She smiled her crooked smile, continuing in a low voice, "And I'm not the sort to let a round hole change me."

Alison considered the statement, pushing it around in her mind as she twisted the keys in her fingers. Jess looked into her eyes with an expression so achingly open that it took several long moments for her to realize she was holding her breath. The moment stretched between them like pulled sugar, twisting and reshaping itself in the cool of the evening.

Alison moved forward just far enough to be noticeable, and Jess leaned toward her. Her eyes burned into Alison's. The harsh fluorescent light of the building and the smell of drying motor oil faded away as her world narrowed. The sound of cars on the street drifted to silence and all she could hear was the pounding of blood in her ears. Alison closed her eyes.

She hadn't realized the softness of her own lips until they met Jess's. Now the brush of Jess's mouth against hers heightened all of her senses. She felt the heat of the air in her lungs and the tingle of every nerve-ending in her skin. This was by no means her first kiss, but it was the first in a long time that took her breath away. She focused on the feel of Jess's mouth against her own and fought to capture that feeling. She wanted to hold on to it, preserve it, tuck it away like a memory frozen in amber.

All too soon, Jess pulled back. Alison's body followed for a moment before she could force herself to be still. She opened her eyes and saw Jess's lids flutter open. Her eyes echoed the same shock Alison felt. A wave of longing crashed over her. She wanted to push back into that moment. She wanted to force their lips back together and feel it all over again. Her mind spun with the need, and for one long moment, she thought the dizziness would overwhelm her.

Jess's lips parted with agonizing slowness. Her voice was a ragged whisper when she said, "Goodnight, Ali."

Alison was as surprised as she was pleased to hear her voice was steady when she replied, "Goodnight, Jess."

CHAPTER FIFTEEN

i had a great time last night
Me too. Thank you for dinner.
you're great company when can i see you again
I'll be at the hospital tomorrow. Will you be working?
yes but i meant alone a date
I know what you meant. I was being coy.
you had me worried for a minute ;)
Don't worry. I would love to go out with you again.
free for coffee tonight?
You really have a thing for coffee.
portland
so are you free?
Sorry I'm swamped with work tonight. I have a date with a stack of essays about Christine de Pizan.
you know what would help with that? coffee
Lol! It would, but I won't be leaving my office for hours. I have a Keurig.
im going to pretend you didnt say that

It's not that bad. Okay it is. I shouldn't even be calling it coffee, much less drinking it, but my options are limited.

A knock at the door distracted Alison from her text message conversation. She really should have been working, but talking to Jess was too tempting. A visitor would keep her from both working and texting. She scowled and checked her watch. Her office hours had ended quite a while ago. She should reasonably expect no interruptions, but the knock came again anyway. She stood up with a sigh and a glance at the stack of essays. If she could get rid of her unwelcome guest quickly, she could spare a few more minutes talking to Jess before she really had to buckle down and get to grading.

Given the hour, she expected a colleague so she swapped the happy grin for something more blandly professional. Since she couldn't get the image of Jess's half smile and the feel of her lips out of her head it was a monumental task.

She lost the battle for professionalism the minute she saw her visitor. "Jess! What are you doing here?"

Her hair was a bit more limp than normal and she was wearing the powder-blue scrubs again. There were shadows under her eyes, but her smile was as bright as ever. She held two large paper coffee cups.

She offered Alison a cup and said, "I was in the neighborhood."

Alison raised an eyebrow. "You live and work on the other side of the city, but you were in the neighborhood? And you just happen to have two coffees?"

Jess shrugged. "I get around."

Alison took the cup, her fingers lingering on Jess's. "I see you're still not good at talking to women. Here's a tip, don't tell the woman you're dating that you 'get around.'"

"So we are dating. Good to know."

Alison rolled her eyes and stood back, making way for Jess. As she passed, Alison caught a mix of fabric softener and lemon and that same musky perfume that had been on her hoodie. It made her want to lean in, bury her face in Jess's neck and breathe in every molecule of air around her.

Jess walked to one of the worn wooden chairs in front of the desk and collapsed into it. She peeled the lid off her coffee cup and drank deeply despite the steam rising from it. Alison decided not to return to her own chair. Putting the massive structure of her desk between them held no appeal, so she sat on the top of it, her feet dangling just off the floor. When she turned toward Jess her knee brushed against the loose fabric of her scrubs.

"Long day?" she ventured as she sipped her coffee.

"Very long." Jess put her fingertips to her temple. "A set of twins who were both breech and a mom with preeclampsia. Everybody's whole and healthy, though, so it was a good day."

The coffee was rich and hot and warmed Alison almost as much as Jess's presence. "You know I don't know what any of that means right?"

"Of course. Payback." She knocked her knee playfully against Alison's. "I had to Google Christine de Pizan while carrying two coffees and breaking into a university building after hours."

"What did you find out?"

"French writer. Sort of snarky. Had this crazy notion that women are good for more than just making babies and swooning. Wikipedia basics."

"That's really all you need to know. I should have you grade my essays."

"If it would free up your time, I'm game."

Alison put her half-filled cup down on the desk, pressing her palms into the surface. She could feel the grain of the wood across her skin. "I'm glad you did. Break in with coffee, I mean."

Their eyes met and held one another's for a long minute. Just as the tension rose to a palpable level, Jess said, "Me too."

That feeling was coming back to Alison. Of being picked up and swept off her feet. She reveled in the happiness of it. The swoop of her stomach and the tingle of anticipation were intoxicating, but she had passed the age when losing control was completely fun. Now there was a dread born from the scars of past relationships and the tears of lonely nights mixed in with the joy. Her heart told her this could turn into something profound if she let it. Wisdom told her to be wary.

Something of her doubt must have shown because Jess cleared her throat and sat up a little straighter, moving her body too far away for contact. "So...um...don't you have TAs to do all of this grading for you?"

The happy bubble had burst, and Alison pulled back into herself. "I try not to give them everything. I had this one professor, when I was studying in England, who never read a word I wrote. I could tell. But he was consistently critical of all of my ideas. My research was never detailed enough. My conclusions were always recycled. My writing was stiff. Nothing I did was good enough. It was infuriating. How could he know when he never read my papers? I decided I would never do that to my students. If I'm going to give them constructive criticism I have to form my opinions based on their work."

"Where did you study in England?"

Alison hesitated, but couldn't see a way out of answering. "Oxford."

Jess's coffee cup paused on the way to her mouth. She blinked several times. "Oxford. As in *the* Oxford?"

Alison grinned sheepishly. "The one and only."

"That's impressive." Her cup finally completed its journey to her mouth. "Next you're going to tell me you were a Rhodes Scholar."

Silence hung in the room and Alison became very interested in the pattern of cracks in the fake leather backing of Jess's chair.

After a long moment, Jess nearly shouted, "You were a Rhodes Scholar?"

Alison nodded and shrugged.

"Oh man, I am so outta my league."

"Stop it. I don't really talk about it much. I was turned down when I applied the first time, but they took me after I got my masters at...well..."

Alison nodded toward the wall behind her. Her Master of Arts degree from Harvard nestled between Bachelor of Arts from University of Richmond and her Doctor of Philosophy from Oxford.

Jess's eyes widened as she read the names. She laughed and sat back in her chair. "Harvard? Well, Dr. Reynolds, I am duly impressed."

"Ugh! Don't call me that! I hate it."

"Why? You earned it. I can't imagine Oxford hands those things out to just any pretty face."

Alison's blush deepened, but something in the look Jess gave her made her embarrassment ebb away. "It just feels weird, that's all. I notice you don't like to be called doctor either."

"No. I don't. I thought I would like the way it felt. The acknowledgment of my work, but it doesn't fit me."

"Exactly. I just sort of still feel like I'm nineteen years old, dreaming about what I'm going to do with my life. Like all of this is just make believe. One day it'll all click and I'll be a grown up. Right now, it feels like the department chair is going to walk into this office any day and scream at me to stop messing around and get back to my dorm. I'm not old enough to have a doctorate. I'm not old enough to be shaping young minds. I should be wearing midriff shirts and trying to pass a fake ID!"

"And then go home to play video games?" Jess smiled into her coffee cup. "Believe me, I know exactly what you mean. Something about our generation, maybe. Or maybe everyone feels this way and they don't admit it. We're just kids, we shouldn't have this much responsibility."

Alison bobbed her head in agreement. Her eyes flicked back to the essays on her desk. "Speaking of which…"

"Of course. I'm sorry. I've been keeping you from your work."

"I'm glad you did. I really like spending time with you."

"I really like spending time with you too." Jess's eyes danced as she took a step closer. "More than anyone in a long time."

Alison's heart beat a heavy rhythm against her ribs. "I have a lot of work stuff this week, so I'm not sure when I can see you again."

"It's okay. I actually have a night shift rotation this weekend, so I won't be available either."

"Night shift? Aren't you too important for that?"

"I wish."

"I really will be going by the hospital tomorrow. Maybe we'll see each other?"

Jess took another step, her thigh brushing against the inside of Alison's knee. "It's a date."

Alison realized with a lurch that Jess was going to pass right by her. Her hand shot out and grabbed Jess's wrist. She stopped instantly, clearly waiting for Alison to make a move. If Jess needed her to take the lead, that was fine by her. Her body hummed with the need for contact.

She drew Jess's hand to her waist and slid her own up her arms. Jess's muscles weren't chiseled, but defined and just soft enough. She laced her fingers behind Jess's neck.

"You weren't going to leave without saying good-bye, were you?"

Jess dipped her face down, bringing their lips within inches of each other. "I wouldn't dream of it."

Alison tilted her chin up and their lips met. She assumed their second kiss wouldn't be as overwhelming as the first. Surely the newness had caused the intensity last night. She was so very wrong. She felt light-headed all over again the instant their lips met. Her senses swam and desire coursed through her like a second heartbeat. The giddiness lingered even as time ticked by. She felt the gentle swipe of Jess's tongue on her lips and they flew apart.

Need exploded in her chest as the kiss deepened. There was a sharp intake of breath from Jess and Alison knew she was feeling the same desire. Their tongues danced while Alison slid her fingers into the short hair at the back of Jess's head. The close-cropped hair tickled Alison's fingertips, and she hummed with appreciation. Jess surged forward, pressing the length of her body against Alison and turning her face to fit their mouths closer.

Alison grabbed a fistful of the soft cotton shirt covering Jess's back. The feel of her body was pressing every thought out of Alison's mind. She wanted to kiss her even deeper. To shred her clothing to pieces. To lay back across the papers covering the surface of her desk and to pull Jess's warm, perfect body with her. Jess's body stiffened and shook with the effort of restraining herself.

Alison slid her hand down from Jess's hair past the loose collar of her shirt. The muscles between her shoulder blades bunched at Alison's touch. She spread her fingers wide, trying to soak up the divine feeling of those taut muscles. Several long minutes passed as they discovered the contours of each other's mouths. The pressure building in Alison was becoming impossible to ignore, and she knew she had to stop soon or risk passing a point of no return.

Jess made the decision for her by gently breaking the kiss, but she held her face close to Alison's and kept her eyes firmly shut. Both of their chests heaved from lack of oxygen and the headiness of the moment. Jess opened her eyes and they were like molten emerald.

"I...Um..." Jess swallowed hard and the corner of her mouth twitched just enough to show one bright, white incisor. "Forgive how incredibly lame this is going to sound, but... Wow. I mean...Wow."

Alison laughed, a quiet chuckle that she hoped didn't waver too much as she tried to keep the world from spinning around her. "I agree...Wow."

The air between them thickened, and Alison held her breath. She felt like she was standing on the edge of a cliff, waiting for permission to launch herself into the limitless sky, but not altogether sure she was ready for the risk. Just when the moment pulled fully taut, Jess slowly stood straight. Their bodies separated reluctantly. Alison's hand glided up and over Jess's shoulder, falling into her lap as she finally set her lungs back into motion.

Jess's eyes slid over her just as slowly, and then she shoved her hands deep into her pockets and took another step back, her calves bumping into a chair.

"Well goodnight then. Maybe I'll see you tomorrow?"

"Yeah! Yes...I hope so."

Jess grinned and opened the door, moving through in one quick motion. She looked back over her shoulder with a smile before disappearing behind the closed door.

Alison waited a long minute in case she walked back in, and then sighed and let her feet fall to the floor. The contact shuddering through the bones of her feet was jarring. Like a single off-key note in a song that pulled her irreparably from the moment. She walked around the desk and flung her body into the chair. The tall leather back held her but provided no comfort. She looked at the pile of papers, then at the door and back to the desktop. She noted absently that there wasn't as much clutter on it as usual. There was generally a stack of books and a notepad or two at least, but now it was almost entirely bare. If there was ever a day to drag someone onto it with romantic design, this was that day. She closed her eyes and pictured the scene.

Jess banging the door open and storming back in. Sweeping a powerful arm over the surface of the desk. Pieces of discarded paper fluttering to the ground like a ticker tape parade. Wrapping an arm around Alison's waist, picking her up and depositing her roughly on the cleared surface. Lying down and watching Jess climb on top of her with an animal need burning in her eyes. Trapping Alison beneath her sinewy body. Then lowering herself slowly, ever so slowly, until her weight settled on top of Alison. Alison hooking a knee around her hips. Their lips crashing together, this time with no doubt of what would develop. Jess's body slipping purposefully between her legs. Her hand dipping beneath the fabric of Alison's shirt and moving up over the soft expanse of her stomach. Fingers wrapping around the hem of her skirt and tearing it off with a rip of fabric.

Alison opened her eyes before the fantasy could develop further. Her hands were already shaking. She ran them through her thick curls, and then pulled the stack of papers toward her. The words on the top page refused to come into focus. The bewitching smell unique to Jess hung in the air and, Alison realized with a twist in her gut, on her own clothes. She groaned, dropping her head onto the stack of papers.

It was going to be a very long night indeed.

CHAPTER SIXTEEN

Beth's finger traced the square line of her husband's jaw, the manicured french tip scratching noisily along the stubbly, two-day growth of beard. She giggled, whispering into his ear. His face split in a grin and he whispered back, his broad lips tracing words that only his wife could hear. Their faces were millimeters apart, their mouths almost indecently close to each other. The low murmur of Stephen's voice broke off as he brought Beth's hand to his lips, kissing reverently across the peaks and valleys of her knuckles. She stroked his jaw again, this time letting her finger trail up past his ear into the fringe of his sideburns. His face disappeared from view, past her cheek to the column of her throat. A quiet gasp escaped Beth's lips and white showed under her half-lidded eyes.

Alison took a quick step back out of the doorway. Normally she would tease them relentlessly over their displays of affection. Today, still reeling from Jess's visit to her office, the scene made her squirm. She moved back into the hall where they were out of sight, but her reaction lingered. She reached out a hand to the wall to steady herself, taking a few quick breaths.

She caught a hint of the perfume that was becoming all too familiar, but thought she was imagining it. Her overactive mind conjuring another fantasy. Then the breath of whisper touched her ear, rustling her hair and causing a shiver across the skin of her neck.

"Are they always like that? The nurses say it's like chaperoning the prom in there."

Alison smiled, her stomach performing impressive gymnastics. "Since the moment they met. I cannot begin to tell you all the things I've walked in on."

Jess leaned against the wall beside her. "Well, now I know what we can talk about on our next date."

Alison felt certain she'd gone beet red from her hairline to her collar. She tried to stammer a response, but the sound she made was something like a fish drowning.

"I'm sorry. I made you uncomfortable." Jess stood straight, rubbing her neck and looking like she wanted to melt into the floor. "I was just...trying to be funny. Not good with women remember?"

"No! No! You didn't make me...It's just..." She stopped and took a breath before looking up into those green eyes. The concern in them was almost enough to make her look away again. "I'm sorry. I don't know what's wrong with me today. I guess I didn't get enough sleep."

It was an understatement by half. If she'd slept more than an hour or two it would be a surprise. Thoughts of Jess had flowed through her mind long after she climbed into bed. The feel of her kiss and the warmth of her skin. The way her eyes smoldered. She had buried her face in a pillow, trying to think of something, anything else, but all she could see when she closed her eyes was Jess hovering above her on her desk. Images like that did not lead to sleep.

Now here was Jess, standing not quite close enough and acting so sweet. The squirming in Alison's stomach radiated up to her chest and exploded like fireworks across her skin. She knew she was acting like a teenager with a crush, but it was impossible to stop.

"Are you sure? I know I can be a bit much. I can totally back off if that's what you…"

"Absolutely not. Do not back off." Oblivious to passersby in the hallway, Alison reached out and took Jess's hand. Her skin was soft and slightly pink, like she had just finished washing dishes. "I definitely don't want you to back off."

Jess's smile returned. "Good, because I'm not sure I could actually have done that."

A burst of laughter erupted from Alison before she could stop it.

"Ali? Are you out there spying on us?"

Beth's voice floated through the door behind her and the moment popped like a soap bubble. Jess winked, gave her hand a quick squeeze and turned away. Alison watched her go with a sigh.

"Ali, are you ogling Dr. Jess?" Stephen's voice made her jump. He was standing inches away, grinning at her. "Shame on you for objectifying the good doctor like that!"

"Shh!" Alison pushed him back into the room. "She'll hear you!"

Stephen wrapped a tree-trunk of an arm around her shoulders, dragging her toward the bed. Beth was sitting up, looking distinctly annoyed at the interruption. When she caught sight of the lingering pinkness on Alison's cheeks, her face transformed into a mask of glee.

"Just what have you been up to, Alison Reynolds?"

Stephen squeezed his arm and caught Alison's head in the crook of his elbow. "Trying to get into Jess's pants, that's what."

Alison slapped at his stomach. It felt like a slab of marble under his worn T-shirt. "We were just talking!"

Stephen laughed and released her, slipping around to perch beside Beth and taking her hand in his. "Ali was staring at her butt as she walked away."

Beth raised an eyebrow. "Well, it is a nice butt."

"Careful, you!" Stephen's remark echoed Alison's feelings exactly. "I'll fight her for ya."

"I might enjoy watching that." Beth's hand went back to his cheek and her eyes misted over. "Not to worry love. I think Ali'll take me out first."

Alison sat back, feigning a lack of interest. "I don't know what you're talking about."

Beth's eyes narrowed suspiciously. "You went on another date with her!"

"Wait. What do you mean? There was a date already?" Stephen turned accusing eyes on his wife. "You didn't tell me!"

"I would have, dear, but I needed Ali to figure some things out first. I'm pretty sure she has now."

"I…" Alison's voice raised an octave. "What makes you think we went out?"

Stephen shifted to watch her, too, as Beth explained, ticking the points off one by one. "You're blushing like a fan girl. You can't sit still. Your voice just went into falsetto." She squinted, her eyes scanning. "And you haven't made fun of the two of us for making out. It could only mean one thing."

"Enlighten me, Nancy Drew."

"That's a terrible comparison. You should have said Matlock. You know I love Andy Griffith. All those pastel suits and the sweet old man grin. He had those juries eatin' out of the palm of his hand." She stopped with her mouth wide open, looking into space. "What was I saying?"

"It could only mean one thing."

"Right! It could only mean one thing. She kissed you."

"I…What makes you think that?"

Beth rolled her eyes and looked at Stephen. "She's thinking about them making out right now."

He shrugged at Alison. "Even I can tell that."

Alison huffed and stood up, moving to sit on the foot of the bed. "Okay fine. So it's *possible* we *may* have kissed."

"Of course. Details. Now."

"Oh no!" Alison held up her hands. "I am a lady and a lady does not kiss and tell."

Stephen scoffed. "Yeah right!"

Beth looked stonily at him and his face fell. Alison matched her glare. They crossed their arms over their chests simultaneously. He straightened, fear leaking into his voice. "What? What'd I do? We were…and then you said…and then… How am I in trouble?"

"You aren't in trouble dear." She turned a simpering smile on her husband. "Stephen, sweetheart, why don't you run to the cafeteria and get a soda?"

He looked between the two women, trying to discover at what point he lost control of the situation. "Get a soda? What am I, ten years old?"

Beth patted his hand, and then grabbed a five-dollar bill from her purse. She held it out to him with a smile. "Go get a soda, dear."

"But I want to hear the juicy parts!"

She shoved the bill into his jeans pocket, and then turned his hips toward the door. "Go!"

She smacked him hard on the butt and he hopped a little, walking faster. "The two of you and your objectifications and your…your girls club!"

He turned and winked at Beth when he got to the door. The two women watched him go. When the sounds of the hospital drowned out his footsteps, Alison collapsed across the foot of the bed, her arms outstretched. She let out a whimper.

"That bad?"

Alison could only nod and whimper again. She rolled onto her side, pulling her knees up to her chest. She gave Beth a tortured look over the growing swell of belly between them.

"When did you go on this date?"

"Two nights ago."

"Where to?"

"Bistro Bobette."

"Mmmm. Good taste. Her choice?"

Alison nodded.

"Am I going to have to pry everything out of you? Because Stephen won't be gone forever."

Alison pushed herself up on an elbow. "It was amazing. She was perfect. She likes history. She knows about the Papal

Schism and the Black Death. She does history courses online for fun. For fun! Did you know that's a *thing*? She made me laugh so hard I was practically crying. She paid the whole bill and it didn't piss me off. Then she kissed me goodnight and I don't remember driving home."

Beth purred again. She had a way of making herself understood without words. It was an art Alison had never quite mastered. "Oh, she must be good."

Alison buried her face in the blanket. "I almost threw her across my desk last night."

"Last night? You saw her again last night?"

"She brought me coffee in my office. We were texting and I told her I had to work late and she showed up with the coffee like five minutes later."

"And?"

"And we made out a little. She didn't try anything."

Beth raised an eyebrow. "That's good right? Not making a move. She's after more than just a quick lay. She's treating you with respect."

"I know! And she's so adorably awkward and chivalrous and just thinking about her makes my stomach hurt."

"So you think it's too good to be true."

"She's totally gonna break my heart."

Beth laughed. The sound came straight from her belly and made her whole body shake. Alison stuck out her bottom lip in an exaggerated pout.

Beth finally stopped laughing, wiping tears from her eyes and said, "Ali, you are the only woman I've ever met that sees falling in love as a bad thing."

"I am *not* falling in love! I met her like two weeks ago. It's too soon to fall in love."

"I fell in love with Stephen on our first date." She leaned forward. "And you know good and well that you've already waited longer than we did to go to bed. Live a little! You're too old and too smart to follow all of those outdated rules about dating."

"Nice. My best friend calling me old."

"I've already picked out a nursing home for you. They have bridge on Wednesday nights."

"I hate you."

"You love me and you know it. When do you see her again?"

Alison sighed and sat up, hanging her legs over the bed and letting her feet swing. "Not sure. We couldn't make plans because of work. It'll probably be middle of next week at least."

"You'll die before then. Why not this weekend?"

"She has to work the night shift."

"Then you can take her out for lunch. Take her somewhere casual, get her drunk and she can sleep it off at your place." Her grin was wide as a cat's. "Preferably on top of you."

The idea held a certain appeal. "You are too much. But that's actually a good idea."

"I always have good ideas."

"It probably won't work out. Besides I can wait until next week."

"No, you can't."

"No, I can't."

Beth yawned so wide her jaw cracked. "I suppose there is a chance she'll say no, but if I were you I would change the sheets." She let her eyelids flutter shut. "You know. Just in case."

With her eyes closed, she couldn't see the smile that spread across Alison's face.

CHAPTER SEVENTEEN

"Beth!"

A wall of navy blue scrubs blocked the doorway to Beth's room, and Alison pushed her way through.

"Hey! Wait!" one of them screeched and grabbed her arm.

"It's okay, Nancy." Beth's look was full of reproach, but she had a sheen of sweat on her forehead and a pale ring around her tightly closed mouth. Alison knew all too well what fear looked like on Beth's face, and that she was trying valiantly to disguise it. "What are you doing here Ali?"

"Stephen called me."

"I told him not to call you. You don't need to worry."

Alison dropped her purse on the floor as she hurried to the bed. "He's stuck across town doing an estimate. Someone needs to be here with you."

Beth was lying flat, her pillows stacked neatly on the bedside table. "What about your classes?"

"Jennifer's covering until I get back."

The blankets were pushed down off Beth's belly. A young woman on a stool fiddled with the controls of an ultrasound machine on the other side of the bed.

Nancy marched to the end of the bed. The badge clipped to her lapel rattled, the tag announcing her status as an RN swinging wildly behind it. "We're about to do an ultrasound. Can I ask you to wait outside?"

She may as well not have been in the room for all the notice Alison gave her. She focused completely on Beth. "What's wrong?"

"Nothing's wrong." Beth winced as the ultrasound tech squeezed a large dollop of cold gel onto the crown of her belly. "I've just had some cramping and my heart rate's a little high. Jess says it's nothing to worry about."

"Where is Jess?" Alison turned accusing eyes on Nancy. "Why isn't she here? This is an emergency."

Beth squeezed her hand. "It's not an emergency."

"It's not an emergency," Nancy echoed. She glared at Alison and continued. "The ultrasound is a precaution and her pulse is elevated because she's nervous. We just need to stay calm, right Beth?"

Beth closed her eyes and nodded, taking a couple of deep breaths and blowing them out slowly. "Right. Everything is fine." She opened her eyes, looking a little more relaxed. "There hasn't been any bleeding. The cramping passed quickly. Everything is fine. Jess asked for the ultrasound just so I could see him. It'll help to see him. It will."

"Okay, I'm all set here." The ultrasound tech's voice was little girlishly high. "Are we ready to go?"

Nancy reached for Alison's arm. "Miss, if I could ask you to wait in the hall."

She did not even turn in the nurse's direction. "I'm not going anywhere."

"Can't she stay?" Beth chewed on her bottom lip. She held Alison's hand in a bruising grip. "Please Nancy? Since Stephen can't be here?"

Before Nancy could answer, the technician chirped cheerily, "The more the merrier."

Nancy's scowl showed she didn't agree, but she was outnumbered. Almost the moment the ultrasound wand touched Beth's belly a staticky, underwater sound filled the room.

"Okay little guy, where are ya?" The technician squinted at the monitor. The screen was a blur of black and gray pixels in constant motion as she moved the wand around. She painted lines of clear gel across Beth's stretched skin. "Time for your close-up, buddy. Don't hide."

Alison looked back and forth between the blurred image on the screen and Beth's face. It was pinched with worry, and the longer they waited, the more pinched it became. Alison had never been present for a moment like this. All of the previous miscarriages had been unexpected. Even as the number of them mounted, each doctor had been confident that this new pregnancy would last. The last was always a fluke, something they could correct.

The last doctor had been the first to paint anything but a rosy picture.

That was the lone visit Alison had made with Beth. She remembered the short, stocky woman with wide glasses and hair pinned straight back off her forehead who had barged into the room where she and Beth had been waiting for forty-five minutes. It was just two weeks after her latest miscarriage and the doctor was looking at a clipboard when she entered and barely took her eyes off it when she said Beth's name. Alison had found the chill of her manner sickening.

Not until after Beth had chosen her had she discovered the woman was also a recently elected, extremely conservative state senator. Since her election she had shown a growing disinterest in her medical career, but she had come highly recommended by one of the other attorneys at Beth's firm. The doctor tore her eyes from the clipboard long enough to bark out an explanation about Beth's 'hostile uterus' and 'inadequate placental formation' before flatly declaring that it would be selfish of her to continue attempting to conceive. She would never be able to carry a baby to term and she would doom all of her fetuses to an early death. She left without shaking Beth's hand or scheduling a follow-up appointment. Beth spent the next ten minutes sobbing into Alison's shoulder. The nurse who came to check on them was neither surprised to see her upset nor apologetic for her treatment.

A tear started in the corner of Beth's eye. She stared at the monitor, willing the image of her son to appear there.

Alison turned on Nancy. "Where is Jess?"

"Dr. Baker is in surgery right now."

"She needs to be here."

They squared off across the bed, Alison tightly gripping Beth's hand. "Dr. Baker has a lot of patients and she doesn't have to be present for an ultrasound. She asked me to call her in the OR as soon as it's complete. I don't think…"

"He makes an appearance at last!"

A new sound floated through the static and sloshing. It was difficult to make out at first among all the other sounds, but it soon became more distinct. A rhythmic sort of gurgling noise. Something like slapping a steak on a cutting board or squashing a tomato in your hand.

Beth's voice was a whisper. "Ali."

Tears streamed down her face. The picture on the monitor flashed white and then cleared. Sharpened. The black and gray blob transformed into a black and white blob. Alison squinted at it. There was a tiny spot near one side of the white part that was flashing between gray and white. One small adjustment of the wand and the sound got louder. Stronger.

The tech pointed at the flashing spot with a blue-gloved finger. "Nice steady heartbeat on this little guy."

Everything seemed to come together in a moment. The tech's finger moved away from the white part of the blob and suddenly it wasn't a blob anymore. There was a nose. The big white lobe curled above the flashing pixel was a head. Alison could even see the hint of an eye above the nose. Something moved at the other end. Toes. Tiny toes flexed out at the top of a foot. She looked at the pixel again. It was flashing at the same rate as the wet slappy noise. It was his heart, and it was beating. Dancing in his tiny chest inside her best friend's big belly.

Alison looked over at Beth and she was smiling like she hadn't since the day her baby Rachel was born. Beth turned that beaming smile on her and they laughed together.

"That's your son."

"That's my son."

Alison didn't feel the wetness on her cheeks until she realized the screen was blurry. She wiped her eyes and she could see him again. She watched him stretch his leg out and curl up a little tighter. The tech typed a few commands and Nancy asked her a question or two. It was all lost on Alison. She stared and stared and held Beth's hand.

"Is that him?" Stephen's rich baritone floated across the room, making Alison jump. "Is that our son?"

He was moving into the room like a man who was lost. He fixed his eyes on the monitor. They shined suspiciously.

Beth let go of Alison's hand and held it out for Stephen to take. He hurried to her side and they laughed together through their tears. Stephen leaned over, kissing her cheek and Beth smiled up at him like he was the sun. Alison wished again that Jess were here.

Nancy was glaring at her from across the bed again, and Alison took it as a cue to leave. "I should be getting back to work. I'm glad everything's okay."

Stephen dropped Beth's hand and wrapped his arms around Alison's neck. He smelled like grass and sweat again. There was still something of the sun's warmth clinging to his clothes.

"Thank you for being here when I couldn't, Ali." He smiled through his tears. "I can't tell you how much it means."

"Anytime." She looked over at Beth, who looked ten years younger than when Alison had arrived. "I'll see you this evening to give you your pedicure."

"You don't have to, Ali. You missed work already because of me today."

Alison looked around for her purse. "I know it's hard for you to see your toes these days, but girl, they need help. I'll see you later."

She caught one more malevolent look from Nancy as she stepped into the empty hall.

CHAPTER EIGHTEEN

The sound of that tiny heartbeat echoed in Alison's ears for the rest of the day. She taught her classes, but she saw flashing gray pixels instead of her students' faces. She tried to work on lesson plans, but she was too giddy. Her face hurt from smiling. He was alive. His heart was strong. She wished again that Jess had been in the room to share the moment. She wanted to talk to Jess about the miracle of it. Hold her hand or lean against her body and describe all of the emotions of the day with someone who would see the beauty of it more than anyone.

That happiness made it all the more jarring when she arrived back at Beth's room to find her friend agitated and restless. The morning's scare had unsettled Beth more than she had anticipated, and something of her energy rubbed off on Alison. The abrupt change in her own mood felt like an itchy sweater. She wanted to be rid of it more than anything. She fidgeted in her seat, and nothing they talked about soothed their nerves. When Beth's phone rang, Alison wasn't alone in her relief.

Alison headed for the door. "We'll reschedule your pedicure for tomorrow."

Beth gave her a cold smile and she gladly escaped the room.

"Okay ladies, I'm heading home. Everyone should be okay for the night, but call me if you need me," said a familiar voice at the nurses station.

Alison nearly laughed with relief. Now she could shed the unpleasant tension of her day and replace it with the far more enjoyable tension of asking Jess out on that date.

"Hold on. Before you go Dr. Baker," Nancy barked from behind the counter. Jess stood on the other side, a messenger bag resting against her hip. Alison tried not to stare at the way the strap crossed over her chest, accentuating the lines. "Room eighteen. Her blood pressure?"

"Oh yeah, it's come down a little, but I want her to stay overnight."

"She's not happy about it."

"I know." Jess adjusted the bag and started walking in Alison's direction. "But that'll teach her to eat gas station hot dogs on the way to her prenatal appointment when she's already been warned about her sodium intake. You know my number. See you in the morning."

She turned and her eyes locked on Alison's. She had gotten used to seeing Jess's face split into a wide grin when they saw each other, especially if the meeting was unexpected. This time, however, she looked distracted, and gave Alison the kind of smile you give to an uncle you don't particularly like when he interrupts a conversation at Thanksgiving.

"Fancy meeting you here."

Jess gave a half-hearted laugh and her eyes softened. Clearing her throat, she said, "I was heading out for the day. Can I walk you to your car?"

She caught herself staring at the plump curve of Jess's lips. "Sure. I'm in the deck."

They walked in silence for a few moments, Alison lost in pleasant memories of Jess's lips. Jess still looked distracted, her eyes constantly moving, but never seeming to fall on Alison.

Alison scowled, trying to find a way to break the strange coolness between them. Fate kept conspiring against her today. No matter how much she tried to be happy, everyone around her was grumpy.

Jess coughed, holding the door to the stairwell open. "So, umm…tell me something I don't know about you."

Alison played with the strap of her purse and fixed her eyes on her feet. She climbed a couple of stairs before responding, not bothering to hide the note of sourness Jess's bad mood inspired in her. "I'm an open book. Ask away."

Jess finally looked over, her brows knitting. Alison refused to meet her eyes. "What's your favorite color?"

"Red."

"Hmm. Interesting." When that didn't elicit further comment, she continued, "Coke or Pepsi?"

"Come on, I'm from the South! Coke, of course."

"Wine or beer?"

"Yes, please."

Jess laughed, and Alison smiled at her shoes. "I'll remember that for another day. *Star Wars* or *Star Trek*?"

Alison pushed open the parking deck door, stepping into the maze of cars. "*Star Trek*."

Jess came to a sudden halt. "You have got to be kidding me!"

"Don't ask the question if you aren't prepared for the answer, Dr. Baker."

"That's a 'getting to know you' question you ask because you have to, but there is only one acceptable answer. *Star Wars* brought sci-fi to the mainstream and changed American cinema forever. Come on! R2-D2! Han Solo! The gold bikini! 'Luke, I am your father!' What does *Star Trek* have on that? Nobody could possibly like *Star Trek* over *Star Wars*!"

Alison walked slowly toward her, putting a deliberate sway in her hips. "Well this body likes *Star Trek* better. Patrick Stewart. George Takei. I mean, do you see his Facebook posts? He's hilarious!"

Jess resumed walking, passing Alison without showing the slightest hint of interest. "That's not the shows, that's the actors. Doesn't count."

"What can I say? I have a thing for redshirts."

"Well, you at least get nerd girl points for knowing about the redshirts."

"I found an article called 'Ten Things You Should Know if You're Dating a Nerdy Gamer Girl.'" She was hoping for another laugh, but received awkward silence instead. "I...think it was a Buzzfeed list or something."

They walked in silence. Jess had wandered off again, and Alison was left feeling cold and confused.

Finally she ventured, "How was work?"

"Oh, you know. Large women in pain, tiny angry humans. Lots of blood and screaming from both. Normal day."

"Right."

"I'm sorry." Jess stopped and pinched the bridge of her nose. "It was kind of a long day. I hate that I was stuck in the OR when Beth was getting her ultrasound and Nancy told me...Never mind. I'm not the best company at the moment."

Alison smiled at her, but it felt forced. "It's fine. Been there."

Jess walked on. "I'm looking forward to next week when we can get together again. Email me your schedule so we can find a night that works?"

"Sure. Soon as I get home," Alison said, stopping behind her car and taking a deep breath. "I know you're on nights this week, but maybe I can take you to lunch? I can buy you a burger or something and then get you back home in time to sleep for work. You know, even the score a little. You took me to dinner and coffee. It's my turn. There's this burger place in Carytown...I'm rambling and I'm not even sure why."

Jess smiled, and it was a lot closer to her normal smile this time. "I'd like that. We saw each other at the bar in Carytown, remember?"

"Right. At Babe's. Wait. Did you say yes and I missed it?"

"I did say yes. Lunch sounds great. If you're sure you have the time."

"Great. Yes. I have the time. I'm looking forward to it."

She held her hands behind her and leaned forward just enough to be an invitation rather than an insistence. To her great disappointment, Jess took a step back.

"Definitely."

She took another step and Alison let her shoulders drop.

"Safe trip home."

With that, she turned on her heel and continued down the row. Alison watched until she rounded a corner and was out of sight. Disappointment welled up in her like a bitter cousin of the happiness Jess's presence normally inspired. She shrugged and vowed, as she opened the driver's side door, that she would not let herself dwell on Jess's coldness all night long.

She dropped her forehead to the steering wheel. She didn't stand a chance of living up to that promise.

CHAPTER NINETEEN

"You know what I want, Ali?"

Alison applied another layer of pastel orange nail polish. "To come home from work every night and be greeted by Stephen, naked on your bed holding a bottle of 2003 Chateau Lafite Rothschild in one hand and a million dollars in the other."

"Obviously."

Alison held the brush far away from the nail she just finished while Beth giggled.

"Seriously though. It's something so much simpler." Beth's laughter died slowly, melting into something dark and unbearably sad. The swell of an enormous tear was gathering in the corner of her eye. Alison watched it, sure it would fall any moment, as Beth continued, "I want to go to Labor and Delivery."

"I'm sure you can go over there. We'll snag you a wheelchair and go for a field trip. Where is it?"

"It's upstairs. Just one floor away." The tear hung in her eye, the reflection of fluorescent light dancing on its surface. "And completely out of my reach."

She smiled, and the movement finally knocked the tear loose. It slid down the swell of her cheek, diminishing as it left a trail of itself behind.

"You know that scene they put in like every movie? The woman with the impossibly large belly shouts to her husband that her water broke. He sweeps her up and drags her to the car."

"Of course. It's in every chick flick."

"She screams at him that she forgot her bag and he runs back inside for it. He throws it in the backseat and she yells at him to get her pillow, so he runs back inside for the pillow. Then they go to the hospital, swerving in and out of traffic at ridiculous speeds and pull up to the Emergency Room. They get her a wheelchair and she is huffing, puffing and screaming and they wheel her upstairs."

"You won't watch a movie without that scene," Alison teased.

"That room upstairs. The one where she gives birth to the perfectly healthy, perfectly clean, silent, sleeping cherub. That room is in the Labor and Delivery unit."

She turned to the window and another tear followed the exact same path as the first.

"It's where women go to give birth. It's where they go when everything goes right and when they're done they have a baby."

Alison swallowed with difficulty and watched Beth run a hand over her growing belly.

"I used to have these daydreams of the herd of perfect children with straight teeth and brilliant minds and fairytale weddings and a gaggle of grandchildren. Now all I want is to make it to Labor and Delivery."

"Bethie…"

"Do you remember when I had Rachel?" There was a pleading in Beth's eyes that Alison couldn't ignore. She nodded and Beth continued. "We had that movie moment. Stephen and I. My water broke and we ran to the car. I sent him back in for more pillows because I knew there wouldn't be enough. He thought he could get away with only one."

"He's always been cuter than he is smart."

Beth smiled at her joke, and the tears seemed to have stopped. She looked out the window again, her hand stroking her belly almost absently. Alison screwed the top back onto the bottle of polish more to have something to do with her hands than anything else.

"Ignore me, Ali. I've been stuck in this bed too long." The corners of her lips turned up the same way they had when they were kids and she snuck a piece of chocolate from her mom's kitchen. It was unsweetened baking chocolate, but Beth ate it all the same and pretended to love it. "Too much time to think. Still…I wonder what it looks like up there. I wonder what color the wallpaper is."

Before Alison could think of anything to say, there was a loud knock. A nurse she hadn't seen before swept into the room.

"Sorry to interrupt the chat ladies, but it's time for me to get your vitals and visiting hours end in five minutes."

Alison glanced at her watch, but didn't see where the hands were pointing through gathering tears. She kissed Beth's cheek, collected her things and nearly ran for the door. She couldn't tell whether she was about to throw up or cry. Both seemed quite likely. The urge to drop her bag, kick off her shoes and sprint for the elevators was difficult to overcome. She and Beth had a nearly perfect track record of, if not fixing each other's problems, at least knowing how to make each other feel better. The longer this pregnancy stretched, the less Alison was able to contend with Beth's feelings or her own.

Passing the last room on the hall, she heard a whisper of Jess's voice. She picked up her pace and ducked into the stairwell before she could be seen. Even the briefest flash of that winning smile right now and she knew exactly what would happen. She would pull Jess into a storage closet and rip every stitch of clothing off her body. She would bury her fear and doubt in Jess's body and ruin everything. The sex would be amazing and she would feel so good while it lasted. And she would also smash the fragile framework of something special into a million pieces.

She leaned against the metal railing of the stairwell and took several deep breaths. Her palms caught on the uneven surface.

The top layer of paint on the railing was red, but was worn thin in areas and chipped in others, showing innumerable layers underneath, each a different color.

She imagined the thousands of people who must have stood in this very spot and gripped this very railing. What color had it been when they held it? Were they crying from bad news or laughing because of a triumph? Most were probably somewhere in between. Holding this metal for the mere fact of needing something to hold on to.

Or perhaps they had no idea where their hands were resting. They had shared this space with her, but in a different time, and were completely unaware of any significance. Most people were. Even the most important moments usually involved people who had no idea that they were a part of history. People who had not intended to make history and instead found it being made around them. Those were the people who brought Alison to the world of history when she was young and they were the ones who would always keep her there.

Alison studied the flight of stairs. They could take her up to Labor and Delivery right now. She could see that place and tell Beth that it wasn't all that great. All pastel blues and pinks on the walls and furniture. It would be filled with the sounds of babies and mothers.

She turned away and started walking down the stairs. They would take her to her car and her home and tomorrow she would know what to say to Beth to make her happy again. She wouldn't go to Labor and Delivery. Not yet. Not without Beth.

CHAPTER TWENTY

"Why history?"

The room around them was bustling with noise, but Jess and Alison's table sat far enough into the corner of the restaurant that it was only a dull buzz outside of their bubble. The restaurant was one of Alison's favorite places, Burger Bach, just outside of the fashionable Carytown area. It hadn't occurred to either of them that it was a Saturday afternoon in the fall, which meant college football and loud, drunk fans. Still, the waiter who met them at the door gave them a knowing look and seated them in the quietest corner booth available. He handed over menus with a wink before he sashayed off.

"*God Speed!*"

Jess picked up a french fry. "Am I going somewhere?"

"By Edmund Blair Leighton." Alison smiled at her half-empty plate. "When I was a kid, eleven or twelve I think, we went on a school field trip to the Smithsonian. A very prim and proper line of private school girls tiptoeing through this massive art museum. They had a special exhibit that day and there were several paintings by Edmund Blair Leighton. *The Accolade, Stitching the Standard, Tristan and Isolde*. The one that really got me was *God Speed!*"

Jess picked up her glass and eyed the contents. She had chosen a bottle of Hardywood Brewery's Coffee Stout because, she said, they were the only decent local brewery. It was infused with roasted beans from Lamplighter, one of the only coffees in town that she liked, and it carried the pleasant memories of their first date. The beer was heavy, heady and thick as chocolate milk going down. The day outside was just cool enough to warrant the heaviness, and the flavor was bold enough to stand up to her burger made of ground lamb and piled high with goat cheese and spinach.

"That makes sense. I'll admit, when we met I guessed you did something more in the arts field."

"It's the skirts isn't it? I give off an artsy, hippie vibe even if it doesn't fit me at all."

Jess wiped creamy suds from her upper lip with her napkin. "I wouldn't say it doesn't fit you. You just seem like a person who is more into…I don't know…characters? People rather than memorizing dates and battle names and all that. But I still don't see how a painting got you into history."

Alison had taken Jess's advice and ordered another bottle from Hardywood. A Peach Tripel that was exactly what she liked. Not too hoppy, not too fruity but with a hint of both. It was smooth. Maybe a little too smooth. Jess's presence was beginning to have an effect on her, so the addition of an easy-drinking, high alcohol beer put her in a dangerously flirtatious mood.

"The painting is one of those romanticized scenes of medieval life. It's a woman tying her scarf around the arm of her knight. He's in full armor, sitting on his warhorse, headed off to battle."

A particularly loud cheer from the bar distracted her, and she looked over her shoulder without really seeing the crowd. Instead she saw a young version of herself, standing in front of a massive gilt frame, staring at that fictional couple. She turned back around to see Jess watching her and the temperature in the room seemed to ratchet up a few degrees.

"Um…I loved it. I couldn't stop wondering about those two. What were their lives like? What was their love like? The plaque beside the painting mentioned courtly love. When I got home, I went straight to the library to research it. I was enthralled. I guess I have been ever since."

Jess shuffled around the few leftover fries on her plate. "Typical woman. Looking for a knight in shining armor. Tell me about courtly love. I feel like it was mentioned in my lectures, but they got very heavy on military stuff and I might have been too bored to pay much attention."

"Hmm. Short attention span." She smiled widely at Jess and was pleased to see her blush a little. "It's all about nobility, purity and acts of service. The most famous example is Lancelot and Guinevere. A knight loves a woman, usually one in a loveless marriage, from afar. He isn't willing to sully her honor by actually seducing her and she is determined to be a proper wife and remain faithful. Then he performs heroic acts and they can't deny themselves anymore. They fall into bed, but forgive themselves because they held out against temptation for a little while. Typical romance novel stuff. Exactly the kind of thing that makes a pre-teen girl swoon."

"Then that pre-teen girl grows up and discovers that chivalry is dead."

"Even worse, she discovers chivalry never existed." She found her fingertips tracing along the lines of Jess's hand where it lay on the tabletop. "Real chivalry was more than just holding open doors and showing up with flowers. And it wasn't just keeping your lady safe, but doing the impossible for her."

"Doing the impossible?"

"A knight was not worthy of his lady unless he could literally slay a dragon for her. With a spoon if that's what she wanted." She lowered her eyes, finally noticing what her hand was doing. A tingle shot through her body as if Jess's skin were electrifying her. "Whatever his lady wanted he was honor bound to make happen, even if he died in the process."

The hand under Alison's fingertips went rigid, but the beer was swimming in her blood and she hardly noticed as she finished, "It's an unrealistic dream."

Jess slipped her hand out from underneath Alison's, reaching for her beer. She took a long swallow and couldn't see the disappointed look on Alison's face through the murky liquid. Jess said, "But it's still your dream."

"Hmm?"

"That's why you love history, isn't it?" Jess's voice held an edge of sharp stone. "You still dream of finding your unrealistic knight in shining armor."

"Doesn't everyone?" Alison reeled her thoughts back, dragging her eyes away from the curve of Jess's neck. It occurred to her how many times she had used male pronouns and thought she understood the chill that had come over Jess. "Although I like the idea of having my very own Joan of Arc even more."

Jess nodded, looking into her beer, her hand firmly wrapped around the glass. Alison frowned. Her joke hadn't smoothed the tension, but she couldn't ask why. She fiddled with one of her rings, the alcohol coursing through her suddenly making her feel a little ill instead of giddy.

"Can I get these plates out of your way?"

The waiter was back, his encouraging smile still firmly in place. There was the slightest bob to his impressively high pompadour as he settled his weight onto one hip.

"Yeah absolutely!" Jess was grinning when she pushed the remains of her lunch toward him. She turned back to Alison and winked. "Want anything else? Another beer?"

Alison stared into her green eyes, alight and happy, and wondered if she'd imagined the awkward moment. "No, I better not."

He left with their plates. Alison didn't want to lose the moment, so she asked, "How about you?"

"How about me what?"

"Why medicine?"

"You mean other than the endless schooling, crushing student loan debt and astronomical malpractice insurance costs? Why *not* medicine?"

"Well, when you put it like that."

This time it was Jess who reached out. She took the hand Alison was using to spin her ring and ran a broad thumb over her palm. A shiver rippled through Alison's body at the touch, but Jess was talking again and she forced herself to listen.

"I'd love to say it was some sort of crusade. Like someone close to me had trouble conceiving, or to make sure that the LGBT community was better served or something like that. Truth is, I just wanted to be a doctor. Ever since I was a kid."

She traced the pale blue path of the veins on Alison's palm and up to her wrist, smiling at her memory.

"When I was little we went to all of these weird swap meets and flea markets and stuff. Mom raised bees and she sold honey there. This one time I kind of wandered off and found this lady selling stuff she'd bought at an auction when a school closed."

"How old were you?"

"Eight or nine maybe."

"And already a rebel."

Jess laughed. "Yeah. You ever see anatomy mannequins? They were kinda creepy actually. Clear human form and inside were these organs. All bright, primary colors. You could take them out to look at and then they clicked back into place. Not exactly accurate anatomically, but enough to teach a kid the general layout of our innards and guts."

"What a great toy. Sounds like the stuff of nightmares."

"Pretty much. Especially just standing in the back of science classrooms. I badgered my mom into letting me buy it with some birthday money I had tucked away. I played with that thing for hours. I could dissect it and put it back together with my eyes closed."

"And you didn't grow up to be a serial killer."

"Not yet. I'm too much of a nerd I guess. All I wanted was to learn what all those neon pieces of plastic were for."

"I guess it was a good toy then."

The sensitive flesh of Alison's wrist tingled from the soft brush of Jess's thumb. Her touch was delicate in a way that made Alison's whole body feel loose and shaky. As much as she craved that feeling, it was overwhelming given the setting. She repositioned her hand, catching Jess's fingers between her own.

"The kidneys got me hooked. Imagine a nine-year-old figuring out her whole life because she liked trying to say glomerulus."

"Glom what?"

"Glomerulus. It's a tuft of capillaries in the kidneys. Helps filter the blood. It's so weird-looking. Like a ball of yarn. Anyway, I was all set to become a nephrologist, a kidney specialist."

"But you aren't."

"Nope. I started med school and something about gynecology and obstetrics just clicked with me. Turns out I was good with figuring out women's bodies. I know. I know. Start with the jokes."

"Oh, I wouldn't dream of it."

Jess laughed that throaty laugh again. The waiter slid their check onto the tabletop between them. Alison released Jess's hand reluctantly to fish out her wallet. She threw a couple of bills down, and as they stood Jess's hand found its way to the small of Alison's back. It rested there lightly, and her heart skipped at the possessiveness of the gesture.

The sun was high and bright after the dim restaurant. Alison worked on a script to casually invite Jess over to her apartment while they walked across the crowded parking lot. Her mouth was watering at the thought of the long walk up to her front door. The shy look she would give as she leaned close. The words she would whisper before wrapping her teeth around Jess's earlobe. She nearly walked into a parked car, but Jess's hand on her back steered her out of the way just in time.

"I would insist on buying you ice cream or something," Jess said as they approached her car. "But I have some stuff to do back home before I sleep."

Alison's stomach plummeted. Pulling the corners of her mouth up into something resembling a smile was harder than she had imagined. "Oh. That's too bad." She saw something in Jess's look that she hoped was regret or at least disappointment. "I'll take a rain check."

Jess didn't respond with words. Instead, she leaned in with a confidence that Alison had not seen from her before. Kissing had become more comfortable between them now. As though they'd been doing it for years and knew exactly how to move together. Alison's hands were on her shoulders, pulling her closer. Jess leaned in, but not indecently close considering they were in a very public and visible spot. Alison melted into the kiss, fully aware that her slight intoxication was doing her no favors in coordination, but not really caring. She felt Jess's chest press against hers. She ached to eliminate all the barriers between them.

She slid her hand experimentally up Jess's side, hoping for some encouragement, but it was clear that Jess was holding back, and Alison hoped it was only because of the lack of privacy. The kiss was full of the promise of more, but it was also restrained. Superficial. It ended much too soon, but she was still thrilled to see the glaze over Jess's eyes.

"I should go. Thank you for lunch."

CHAPTER TWENTY-ONE

How's your day going?
pretty awful yours?
Not bad. How about a drink to make it better?
cant sorry working late tonight
Looking forward to going home and rescuing a princess?
More like blowing up a few dozen aliens
That could be fun too.
id rather see you
Do you get a break any time soon?
god yes any time really we docs can do whatever we want didnt you know that ;)
you thinkin of coming to bust me out of this place?
Maybe.
im your willing coconspirator you bring the beer ill find a chainsaw

That was how Alison and Jess ended up watching the sunset over downtown from the roof of the hospital. Alison had whisked Jess away from the nurses station, but Jess was the one who took her hand and led her up a back stairwell. The stairs ended in a locked door, its key hidden not so secretly over the metal doorframe.

Most of the nurses and a few doctors knew about the roof access. People used it as a place to escape the stress of the hospital, Jess explained, or a place to indulge in the cigarettes that were forbidden throughout the campus. There was an unspoken rule that if the door was unlocked when you got there, the roof had already been claimed and you had to find somewhere else to go. Fortunately, the key was still in place, the hideout was unoccupied, and they could spend some time together away from prying eyes.

An old, mismatched pair of folding lawn chairs waited by the railing. When they sat, Alison reached into her bag.

"You know I was just joking, right?" Jess said with a nervous laugh. "I can't actually have beer while I'm on the clock."

Alison's smile widened and she pulled out a pair of dark brown bottles. She twisted the cap off one and handed it to Jess. The smell of sassafras hit her even through the swirling wind.

"Root beer." She laughed and took an experimental sip. "I haven't had this since I was a kid."

"I brought Coke, too, if you'd rather. The root beer was really just a joke."

Jess put her feet up on the railing. "No, this is perfect. Thank you."

Alison leaned back into her chair, pulling her knees up against her chest. "You're welcome." She drank from her own bottle and looked out over the view. "Why has your day been awful?"

Jess waved her hand and took another drink. "Nothing big, just…You know, I don't really want to talk about it. Tell me about your day instead."

"Okay." Alison let the bottle hang from the end of her fingers, swinging in the air between them. "Let's see, my morning class was non-majors, and they actually seem to be interested. I just can't quite maintain a good balance between lecture and discussion with them. It's like they think they signed up for one of those intro level classes with a few hundred students in a big, theater-style lecture hall. The ones where the teacher drones on endlessly with a slide show in the background. They just want to sit back and take notes, but that's not how my classes are."

"Really? I thought most history classes were like that. I remember having to take one of those my freshman year."

"Did you like it?"

"It was at eight a.m. and I was allowed processed foods and canned beer for the first time in my life. I slept through every class."

"Exactly why I hate them! You probably don't remember a thing from the class, do you?"

"All I remember from that class was Megan Collins."

"Megan Collins?"

Jess set her bottle down on the roof and put her hands behind her head. Alison was so intent on the way her delicate fingers intertwined that she nearly missed her words.

"She was another pre-med and very…distracting. Long blond hair, ripped jeans, punk band T-shirts. The whole nine. I crushed on her almost my entire freshman year."

"Mmm hmmm," Alison purred, sitting forward. "Typical freshman lesbian. What changed?"

"She invited me to a party." The sun had sunk lower in the sky, and Jess kept her eyes on the orange undersides of the clouds. "I thought she was asking me out. She may have been. I never found out. She dragged me to one of the bedrooms in the back of this house. I thought 'This is it!' She sat down on a beanbag chair and dragged me onto the carpet next to her. Then she dropped some acid and went into her own little world. After a half hour of watching her talk to shadows, I got up and left the party. She had no idea. The next day she didn't even remember inviting me. Kind of a turnoff."

"Weren't your parents hippies? I didn't think drugs would bother you."

"They don't. As long as the people doing them can handle it, which most can't. My folks smoked their fair share of weed. I did, too, when I was a kid, but never enough to affect my life.

This girl was super smart and still got terrible grades. She let the drugs ruin her life. I see a big difference between weed and hard-core drugs. I don't know if that makes me a hypocrite or pretentious or what, but I know that Megan Collins came back from spring break with track marks and the clap, and she didn't come back for sophomore year at all."

"Yeah," Alison replied, looking at her feet. "I see that more than I like to admit in my own students."

"I brought the energy down. Sorry. Tell me about the rest of your classes."

"Only two today. That one and a graduate level seminar. I have a good set of grads this semester. Not as good as my doctoral candidate, but they have some lively discussions." She spun the bottle in her hands. "You met my doctoral candidate, actually. She was at Babe's that night. Jennifer."

"The couple playing volleyball, right?" Jess leaned back in her chair, the front two legs lifting off the roof with a crunch of gravel. "The one who tackled her girlfriend right there in front of the whole crowd."

Alison laughed, nodding. "Yeah. Jennifer and Courtney. They appreciate an audience. Courtney is an artist. She does this really amazing mixed media stuff. Mainly…"

Her words trailed off as a shrill electronic beeping cut the evening air. Jess scowled at her beeper for a moment and then turned back to Alison. "You were saying?"

"Nothing." Alison stood, starting to gather her things. "I should let you go."

"No!" Jess shot to her feet, her chair wobbling unsteadily behind her. "I've got time."

She reached out and took Alison's hand. Her fingertips traveled the length of her palm up to her wrist. They lay lightly against the skin there and Alison wondered if Jess could feel how her pulse had picked up at the touch.

"Don't go yet." Jess looked around, her gaze falling where slashes of salmon, orange and red twilight were reflecting on the buildings all around them. She pointed off toward a hill in the distance with a neat line of row houses climbing up it. "Tell me something about Richmond that'll make me like it here more. What's that part of town over there?"

. Alison followed her pointing finger, trying to focus on the skyline rather than Jess's touch on her skin. "That's Church Hill."

"That's right. I've heard people talk about it. Tell me about it?"

Jess leaned back against the railing, holding onto Alison's hand.

"So it's kind of a mix of neighborhoods really. There are some very nice areas with rich people and nice restaurants. Then there are some terrible parts with historically high crime and low-income residents. Also, one of the best bakeries in Richmond."

Jess slid along the railing, wedging her body in between the barrier and the soft curves of Alison's form. "Why's it called Church Hill?"

"Because of Patrick Henry." She leaned into Jess, wrapping her arms around her neck. "You can't really see it from here, but right off in that direction is St. John's Episcopal Church, the spot where Patrick Henry gave his 'Give me liberty or give me death' speech."

Jess dipped her head, her lips dancing along Alison's throat. "Which speech?"

Alison closed her eyes, relishing the feel of Jess's kisses. "What? They don't teach you American history in Portland?"

"American history, yes."

Alison leaned further in, letting her full weight settle against Jess's lean body, pinning her to the railing.

"Virginia history, not really. Other than, you know, slaughtered Native Americans, lots of slaves, bad side of the Civil War, lots of coal."

Jess's lips trailed back down to Alison's shoulder, making her voice came out in a breathy whisper. "The coal is West Virginia."

"They aren't part of regular Virginia? Hmm, good to know."

As Alison laughed, Jess's hand strayed to the hem of her shirt, pausing for a heartbeat before slipping under the fabric. Alison gasped when Jess's fingers, chilled by the air on the windy rooftop, touched her side. A wave of gooseflesh radiated out over her abdomen. She finally pulled Jess's lips up to meet her own and they kissed deeply while the light from the setting sun dimmed.

She pulled back and spoke low, making sure that her lips brushed against Jess's ear when she said, "You're a real jerk about my home state."

"This would be a good time to admit that you find it charming."

She turned her face into Jess's neck. The hand on her side slid slowly up, dancing over her ribs one at a time. Alison dipped her head to press a kiss against Jess's collarbone. Just as her lips were about to meet skin, the electronic chirp chimed again from Jess's waist. She let her hand slip from under Alison's shirt as she reached for it. Alison's breath came out as a sigh.

The light was fading precipitously now, the sun slipping behind a building off to her right, and the salmon and pink in the sky had coalesced into a blood red tinged with deepest purple. Jess scowled at the pager in her hand, silencing it with an unnecessarily firm stab at the button. Alison started to move away, but Jess gripped her waist and held their bodies locked together.

The smile returned to Alison's lips and she said, "You know the most interesting story about Church Hill?"

Jess's voice was alluringly low when she replied, "What's that?"

"There was a railroad tunnel that cut through it. Carved out under the hill itself."

Jess's hand slid back up her side, the heat of her skin registering in the cool night air so high up above the streets.

"One day the tunnel collapsed on a work train that was inside doing repairs. There were a handful of people on the train. Railroad employees. The rescuers tried to burrow in to save them, but it just collapsed even more around them. In the end they had to seal off the tunnel with the train and some of the workers inside."

Jess's lips found her neck again and a flood of longing coursed through her. She squeezed her eyes shut against the intimacy that kept her teetering on the edge of madness. She had longed for this moment, dreamed of it nearly every night since they had shared coffee on that moonlit patio.

Now, finally, Jess's hand slipped over the lightly padded cotton of her bra to cup her breast. She used the most delicate, teasing touch and Alison worried she would crumble apart and be swept away by the sharp breeze. She held Jess's shoulders as much to hold herself up as anything else. Her mind slipped from the story, settling instead on the far more intriguing question of how far Jess would be willing to go this time.

Jess's mouth left her skin. "You were saying?"

"I…What?"

Jess's body was barely visible in the darkness, but the teasing smile in her voice was unmistakable.

"The story?" Her hand caressed Alison beneath her shirt. "The tunnel?"

She swallowed hard and forced herself to continue.

"Right. There's an urban legend about it. Some people saw a hideous creature run away from the collapse."

She took another breath. It didn't do much to settle her.

"A huge figure. Taller than any man. With jagged teeth and torn skin. Covered in blood and wailing this inhuman shriek."

Jess slid her other hand under Alison's shirt, cupping Alison's other breast.

"He ran from the tunnel and toward the river, but he was chased by a pack of men. The creature hid in one of the mausoleums in a cemetery overlooking the river."

Jess teased her though the fabric of her bra, and she couldn't hold back a quiet moan. The light from the dying sun reflecting off Jess's teeth as her lip stretched in that crooked smile.

"They…They say it was a vampire who attacked the men. That he caused the collapse to cover his frenzied feeding. That he roams all over the streets of Richmond. Usually he's seen lurking around the two sealed entrances to the tunnel."

Alison struggled to keep hold of her story, but Jess's nimble fingers were fast becoming her sole focus.

"People have quietly gone missing from the area for decades. Victims of the vampire."

Jess's hand left her breast and slid down, over the dips and swells of her chest and stomach. She spoke just as her fingers caught the waistband of Alison's skirt. "A vampire? How interesting…"

Jess tugged lightly on her skirt, drawing the waistband away from her body millimeter by agonizing millimeter. The heat coming off her was mesmerizing. The right side of her lab coat slipped forward, brushing against the exposed surface of Alison's stomach and her breath caught.

Jess's pager went off for a third time. She groaned and her body slumped under Alison, falling back against the ice-cold railing. She released the tension on Alison's skirt, placing it carefully back against her body and withdrew her wandering hands.

"I'm sorry. I really have to go."

All the air went out of Alison's lungs, her whole body sagging. Opening her eyes reluctantly, she saw the reflection of her own disappointment in Jess's features.

"I understand. I've been keeping you from your work."

"I really am sorry."

She forced a smile and tried desperately to rein in her desire. "I know."

The metal door clanged shut behind them. Alison pressed her palms against each other, pushing away the need that still gripped her. They went back down the stairs and out into the halls of the hospital in silence. Before they could say a proper good-bye when they got back to the unit, Nancy grabbed Jess and started chattering at her about some missed phone calls. Alison slipped past the two without a word and hurried on to Beth's room. She thought she could feel Jess's eyes on her as she walked away, but it may have been wishful thinking. Still, she put a little extra sway in her hips, just in case.

She knocked on the doorframe of Beth's room and silently counted to five before rounding the corner. Stephen was bent over the bed, his face suggestively close to his wife. He turned to Alison with a smile that was all broad teeth and waggling eyebrows. She leaned against the doorframe and rolled her eyes hoping that the evidence of her own encounter wasn't as obvious on her features as they were on Beth's. Miraculously, the two seemed too focused on each other to notice her jerky movements and labored breathing.

"You two need to get a room."

"We have one," Stephen said, pointing at the walls around them. "The problem is that people keep walking into it."

Beth scooted up the bed, wincing slightly as her back creaked. "This is the most privacy we've had since Rachel was born. You have no idea how difficult it is to get a little alone time with a two-year-old in the house."

"Speaking of our two-year-old..." Stephen stood and grabbed his jacket off the back of the visitor's chair. "I should go pick her up. When I'm late your parents stuff her full of soda and chocolate and leave her so wired she won't go to bed. It's sneaky, their payback, but very, very effective."

He leaned over Beth and kissed her on the forehead. She closed her eyes and smiled at the touch of his lips, and Alison turned to look out the door. Jess hadn't kissed her good-bye before they left the roof. Suddenly it felt like a torturous oversight. She felt Stephen's hand on her shoulder. He pulled her into a hug as usual, but she wasn't in the frame of mind to appreciate his affection. Her body was still buzzing from Jess's touch, and she didn't want to feel anyone else's until it settled down. He pulled back quickly and gave her a smile before leaving. Jess was standing at the nurses station, pretending not to be spying into the room. Stephen stopped to say a few quick words to her on his way out.

When Alison spent a little too long watching the exchange, Beth clucked. "If you want to make me jealous, you're doing a great job."

"What?" Alison turned back to the room. Her best friend's left eyebrow arched up in a graceful curve. "Oh. Sorry."

"You're so not sorry."

Her smile was so wide it made her cheeks ache. "No. I'm not sorry at all."

Beth patted the armrest of the visitor's chair, and barely waited for Alison to sit before she started in. "So let's just skip the part where I pretend not to know that you came here over an hour ago and ran off with my doctor somewhere to hook up. Okay? Instead we're going to start with all the details."

"Do you have spies following me? How did you know I was here?"

"Ali, sweetheart, you know I can see the nurses station from here, don't you?"

"Right." She pulled her knees up to her chest. Jess was still within sight, but focused on her phone call, looking down as she scribbled notes. "We were texting. She said she'd had a bad day and I decided to come cheer her up."

Beth turned awkwardly on the bed, resting her chin in her hand. "Uh-huh."

"She said she wanted a drink, so I smuggled in some root beer." Beth giggled and she shrugged. Outside the room, Jess's brow furrowed. She spoke quickly into the phone, clicking her pen on the counter in a silent staccato. "We went up to the roof and watched the sun set."

Beth let out a noise somewhere between a whimper and a sigh. "What'd you talk about?"

"She asked about my day. I told her about my classes."

"She asked you about your day and actually listened to the answer? I'll need her to teach Stephen that trick. What else?"

Jess hung up, but kept writing. Alison decided she wanted to keep their moment to herself for a while. She wasn't sure what prompted the reluctance to share, since she never had kept anything from Beth before, but she followed the instinct.

"Nothing really."

Beth followed her eyes out into the hallway. "How much groping was there this time with the kissing?"

The smile slid off her face as she tried hard to sell the lie. "None."

"*What?*"

Jess flipped shut the pastel green cover on the chart she had been working on and handed it to Nancy across the counter. Alison swatted at Beth's arm but missed by a mile. "Shh! God, you are the worst! She's going to hear you!"

"She needs to hear me! This qualifies as torture."

"I think I'll survive."

"I'm not talking about you. I'm talking about me. She needs to get a move on."

"Sorry to interrupt, ladies." Jess tapped lightly on the door, her eyes fixed on Alison. "I won't take more than a minute of your time. Beth, there are a few tests I want to run in the morning if you're up for it?"

Even when she felt Beth's mood shift, Alison couldn't keep herself from staring back into those green eyes. They were sparkling tonight and Alison hoped she was the reason.

"Is something wrong?"

"No. No. Just a little spike in your labs that I want to follow up on." Her voice wavered just for an instant, as if she really had no interest in the discussion. "I just thought you might want to fill Stephen in is all."

"Nice of you to take a break from your work and come in here just for my husband's sake."

Jess blushed and finally tore her eyes away from Alison to stare at the floor. "I just want to keep you informed."

"That's so kind of you, Jess. Thank you." After a pause during which she shot Alison a conspiratorial look she said with a purr, "You're here awfully late tonight."

"I got a little behind." She moved farther into the room and her eyes were back on Alison. "I have the weekend off. Just wanted to make sure to get in a checkup with some of my trouble cases before I disappear for a few days."

Beth tried to catch Alison's eye, but she was too busy staring at Jess. "You have the weekend off? Any plans?"

That caught Alison's attention. She snapped her gaze to Beth, trying to give her a warning, but looking more excited than anything else.

"I don't have any plans." She smiled this time when she looked at Alison. "Not yet, anyway."

Beth put a long finger to her chin, tapping thoughtfully with her manicured nail. "You know what you need? An introduction to Virginia." Her gaze slipped to Alison for the briefest moment. "Since you just moved here and all. You should get to know the place."

"I've heard there's some nice spots on the river. I'd thought about..."

"Not the river." Her voice was so liquid smooth that her dismissiveness didn't even come across as rude. "It's not the right season. Save that for the summer. Fall means mountains around here. They won't be anything compared to what you're used to from the west coast, of course, but the foliage is beautiful."

"I've heard the leaves can be nice this time of year."

A scheming light flashed in Beth's eyes. "You haven't had a weekend off in a long time. You need something relaxing... indulgent." She paused and snapped her fingers. "You should go to a winery! There are some wonderful wineries up in Charlottesville. It's not that far away, right at the foot of the mountains."

Jess shook her head and laughed. "I do love wine." She shot Alison a wink. "Even if I am usually more of a beer person."

"Well, that settles it. You should go visit a winery this weekend!"

With the air of someone playing along when they know they've been tricked, Jess said, "That's not exactly the kind of trip a person wants to take alone."

"I absolutely agree!" Beth scowled theatrically. "You need an enthusiastic partner to share the experience with. Someone who can whet your appetite for adventure and deepen your enjoyment of the experience. I would volunteer, of course. Sadly, my cruel doctor has put me on bed rest so I'm not available to play tour guide."

Alison shook her head. "You're incorrigible, Beth."

"I don't know, Alison." Jess leaned against the end of the bed, clearly enjoying the game. "Your poor friend here is locked up, held at the whim of a terribly cruel doctor. I think it's only right that I should take her suggestion and find the happiness she is denied."

"Not you too!"

"You know, Ali, I just had the most amazing idea!" Beth turned the cheesy smile on her. "You love Virginia. You know all the secret spots. All the hidden treasures that would take her breath away. And the best part, *you're* off this weekend too!"

"I'm a teacher, Beth. I'm off every weekend," she deadpanned. "You just noticed?"

"You're off this weekend, so Jess can play with you." She cleared her throat and started again. "You know how wonderful Virginia wines can be. Maybe she'll gain a new appreciation for the benefits we have to offer if she does a tasting with you."

There was a protracted silence that Beth smiled into, ignoring the squirming discomfort of the other two at the double entendre.

Jess finally spoke up. "I think that's my cue to ask you if you'd like to go to Charlottesville with me on Saturday." She gave a weak laugh and continued, "Although I generally don't have an audience when I ask a woman out on a date, so forgive me for being even more awkward than I normally am."

Despite herself, Alison felt her heart rate pick up. She rested her chin on her knee and answered, "And you'll have to forgive me for having such a meddlesome best friend." Beth just blinked at her and she continued, "I'd love to go. My favorite is Jefferson Vineyards."

"It's a date then. I'll email you so we can make plans. Sound good?"

"Sounds great."

"Then I am going to leave before I start stammering and generally making a fool of myself." She started backing out of the room. "Goodnight!"

She pulled the door shut as she left, and Alison waited exactly three seconds before she stood up and smacked Beth hard on the shoulder. "What is wrong with you?"

"Ouch!" She swatted back, but missed. "Come on, are you really going to pretend to be upset? She just needed a little encouragement, and I was happy to oblige."

"Your hormones are out of control. She doesn't need any encouragement. She asked me out just fine without your help before."

"Yeah, but those were the usual. Coffee, dinner, blah, blah, blah. *This*. Now this date has potential."

"Maybe so. But you are still too much."

Beth lay back, trying to adjust herself to a more comfortable position. "I agree. Anyway, just remember, she has me all lined up for the OR Monday morning. Let her get some sleep. She needs to stay awake for my procedure."

"The date's on Saturday!"

Beth closed her eyes. "Somehow I think Sunday will end up being involved too. Just make sure it's only Sunday morning."

Alison made her way as quietly as she could to the door.

"Oh, and Ali?"

She stopped, her hand halfway to the light switch. "Yeah?"

"You're a terrible liar." She turned onto her side as best she could. "I'll be nice and let you keep whatever happened on the roof to yourself. But only this once."

Alison flicked the light switch off and backed out of the room, pulling the door closed behind her as softly as possible.

"She's always like that, isn't she?"

Alison jumped at the voice so close to her, and Jess put out a steadying hand. She leaned against the wall next to Beth's door. "I'm sorry! I didn't mean to scare you."

Alison pressed a hand to her chest as though she could slow her racing heart with enough pressure. "You startled me is all." She looked over at Jess, who still looked mildly concerned. "I thought you would have run for the hills."

"I've gotten used to her by now. I told you she and Stephen have earned a reputation around here. It's mostly Beth. Pregnancy hormones can be very potent."

Jess stabbed her thumb over her shoulder. "I would offer to walk you to your car, but I'm pretty sure she would flay me alive if I even try to go to the bathroom." But Nancy's attention was elsewhere for once. "Email me later?"

Alison simply nodded. She was suddenly afraid of what she might do if she opened her mouth around Jess. Probably something suited more to the dark and deserted rooftop than an open hallway with a half dozen people around to see. Jess gave her one last dazzling smile before pushing herself off the wall and walking away.

Alison considered it a small victory that she only stumbled once on the way back to her car.

CHAPTER TWENTY-TWO

The picnic was Jess's idea. Alison had described Jefferson Vineyards to her while they planned the date, including the wide expanse of grass near the tasting room. Unlike many of the wineries in the area, the vines at Jefferson were far away from the public buildings. This left a wide lawn that they used for weddings or, as was the case most weekends when it was warm enough, guests who wanted to lounge with their glasses in the sun.

They'd been lucky enough to get fine weather, and Jess suggested they spread out a blanket in a quiet spot and have lunch. The spot they chose was near the bottom of a slight hill. A few mature trees bordered them on the right. A raised platform forming a stage blocked the view from the tasting room behind them. The spot offered the best direct sunlight, but was also secluded. They could hear the chatter and laughter of others from a happy distance. Strangers' voices floated by on the wind. They may as well have been on another planet, Alison thought happily.

Alison and Jess chatted easily while they shared food and a bottle of Meritage. The food was light and refreshing, the wine heavy and dry. The air here on the edge of the mountains was cool, but the sun had decided to grant a few bonus days of warmth before giving way entirely to the changing season and Alison felt it through the thin weave of her sweater and the flowing cotton of her skirt. It made her closed eyelids glow. She lay on her back on top of the coarse blanket, the weight of her curls splayed around her head. She'd finished her glass of wine and put it aside, balanced precariously among the blades of grass.

Opening one eyelid a fraction, she looked at the spot where Jess stretched out. The blanket was small, just wide enough to accommodate the two of them. She hoped Jess had selected it for that reason. Hoped that she craved closeness as much as Alison did. Jess lay propped on one elbow, her eyes scanning the horizon, tracing the distant swell of hills and the jagged tree line, a contented smile on her face.

Alison turned and propped herself up on an elbow, facing Jess. Those green eyes moved from the horizon to her face, and her smile widened. Jess still held her empty wineglass loosely between her fingertips. Those same fingertips that had wandered so agreeably just a couple of days ago. Here in this place, the rest of the world blocked from view, Alison hoped that they would pick up where they left off. As though she had read Alison's mind, Jess leaned back, discarding the glass in the grass behind her.

The movement pulled the sleeve of her black button-up shirt higher, revealing an inch of tattoos. Alison reached out and traced the lines of color with her fingertips. She had meant to ask what they meant, why Jess had gotten them, but as her fingers brushed against her skin, a shiver ran through Jess's body. She traced up Jess's arm, past her shoulder, to the smooth line of her cheek. She eyed the movement of her own hand as her palm settled against Jess's jaw and her thumb caressed her lips. She leaned in and her eyelids fluttered shut.

Their mouths met tentatively at first, just a brush of bottom lips. Jess leaned in, pressing them closer together. The weight of Jess's hand rested on her hip, its solidity comforting even though it maintained the distance between their bodies as much as it increased the intimacy.

Soon Alison was practically melting under her kiss. Any modesty she might normally have felt in such an exposed setting was pressed from her mind by the gentle force of Jess's lips. Her body responded in a flash. She ached for Jess's touch. Ached for the feel of her skin. Ached for the heat so tantalizingly close. Alison leaned in, slipping her hand from Jess's cheek to the back of her neck. The hand around her hip tightened enough to keep her at a safe distance.

Alison didn't want safe. She didn't want distance. Thoughts of Jess had kept her up far too late for far too many nights. The sunlight on her face and the chatter in the near distance were not enough to still her body. She trailed a finger down Jess's throat with the lightest touch. The hand on her hip loosened a fraction. Alison found the top button of Jess's shirt.

The kiss ended abruptly as the sound of conversation came noticeably closer. Jess snapped back, her hand retreating from Alison's hip to her own. Alison looked at her in confusion, but Jess stared over her shoulder, refusing to meet her eye. Alison rolled onto her back, pulling her arms tight around her and staring at the pale blue sky, feeling suddenly cold. A moment later, a middle-aged couple walked past them off to the right. They didn't look over in the direction of the blanket, but continued down the hill hand in hand. Alison shot them daggers as they squatted in the grass a few feet away.

Jess cleared her throat. "It's getting late. We should pack up and head back to town."

Alison frowned, but Jess was already standing up, packing away their glasses, her discomfort over their unwelcome company obvious.

Doubt gnawed at her as they walked back up the hill toward the car. She was acutely aware of the distance between them. Of the way Jess refused to meet her eye. She analyzed the way

Jess had held her, literally, at arm's length when they kissed. Jess tucked the picnic basket in the trunk of her car next to the bottles of wine they'd bought, and Alison moved distractedly to the passenger's door, getting in without waiting for her date.

She got over her uncertainty embarrassingly quickly. How could she not when Jess was so captivating? Not to mention the way Alison's heart started tap dancing against her chest every time she looked over at Jess smiling through the windshield. They hadn't even made it the couple of miles back to the highway before Alison was snorting with laughter at a witticism of Jess's. As the trees whipped by in the median of Interstate 64, they fell back into easy conversation and she settled deeper into her seat. The sun and the wine had made her sleepy, and the whistle of the tires across pavement wasn't helping.

Jess rested her arm on the console between them. Alison reached out impulsively to take it. She wore a ring with a Celtic knot on her right thumb, and Alison pushed her fingers in between Jess's, spinning the ring with her fingertips. Their hands fit together well. Her palm settled against Jess's in a way that felt pleasantly familiar and altogether brand new. Her heart thudded in approval. The swoop in her chest made her bold, and, using the excuse of wanting to examine the ring, she pulled Jess's hand closer.

"What's this?"

"Hmm?"

"The ring. What does it mean?"

"Does it have to mean something?"

One side of the wide band was flattened out of its usual shape and there was a noticeable tarnish to the metal. "It looks like you wear it a lot. Doesn't that have some significance?"

"Just that I like cheap jewelry and intricate designs. I bought it on a whim at a street festival years ago for five bucks. I wear it more out of habit than anything else."

Alison laughed and dropped both of their hands to rest on her thigh with a studied casualness. "How disappointing."

Jess's throat bobbed as she swallowed, but she didn't move her hand. "Should I have lied and said that I'm a leprechaun?"

Alison lounged against the headrest, her eyelids heavy. "I probably would've believed you. You can be very charming, Dr. Baker."

"I do my best."

It was the last thing Alison remembered hearing. The heaviness in her limbs stole over her so quickly that she didn't have time to fight it. One moment she was studying the curve of Jess's jaw, and the next the car was slowing and moving into the exit lane. The bright afternoon sun had mellowed to a deep orange. She sat up with a start and looked around, blinking gumminess from her eyes.

"Shh. It's okay. You fell asleep."

She flushed with embarrassment. Then she felt the weight of Jess's hand still on her thigh. Her own hands had slipped away, but Jess's was still there, resting comfortably just above her knee. Alison's face flushed even redder at the feel of it through the thin cotton.

"Oh, Jess. I'm so sorry!"

"It's okay. Really."

"No it's not. I'm such a jerk."

Jess flashed her another thousand-watt smile as she turned into the quiet residential streets of The Fan. "You're not a jerk at all. I've been totally monopolizing your time practically since the moment we met, your friend is in the hospital and you have a full load of classes to teach. You're allowed to be a little worn out on the weekends."

"Will you stop being so understanding?"

"Not a chance. Sorry."

Alison growled with mock frustration. "Stop apologizing! It makes me feel worse."

Jess smiled and looked over her shoulder to parallel park half a block from Alison's front door. Once she was in the spot, she winked and said, "Sorry."

Alison laughed and leaned across the seat to lay a chaste kiss on her smiling lips. The movement made Jess's hand slip farther down her thigh, but she still didn't remove it.

"Then let me make it up to you." Alison hesitated, anxiety making her voice catch just a bit. "Come up for a glass of wine?"

Jess paused for a heartbeat that lasted at least a century before answering lightly. "Sure. I'll come up for one glass."

CHAPTER TWENTY-THREE

Alison couldn't quite figure out her pace as she climbed the stairs. If she walked too fast, she might seem too eager. Too slow and she would seem uninterested. She noticed every little shift in her own movements, and fretted that Jess could too. She peeked over her shoulder. Jess carried the box of wine in one arm and looked perfectly at ease, her free hand trailing along the banister. Alison's overactive imagination ran through all the possible meanings of Jess's obvious comfort, but no coherent thoughts could attach to each other in the chaos of her mind.

Through some small miracle, they made the journey without rousing Mrs. Crenshaw. Alison fumbled with the keys when she reached the door. Hers was the only apartment on the top floor, and the landing was narrow. She felt Jess's body behind her and forced herself with some effort to focus on the small task of opening the door. Stepping inside and flipping on the light, the familiar space quieted the hum of her body. She looked at the place imagining how Jess was seeing it, hoping she approved.

The living room wasn't much more than a broad rectangle, broken at the far end by a bricked-over fireplace. The mantel over the fireplace was cherry, wonderfully carved and beautifully preserved. It was one of the main reasons Alison lived here. These little architectural oddities added a charm that was missing in the cookie-cutter houses of the suburbs.

Jess clearly noticed the fireplace the moment she walked in. She deposited the box of wine on the coffee table, pulling one bottle out in a single, fluid movement, and walked over to the mantel. She bent to examine the carved filigree.

Alison took advantage to slip into the kitchen. The tiny room, barely big enough to fit the appliances, was tucked away sufficiently to give her a moment to slow her breathing. She hurried to the sink and the small oval mirror hanging above it. The face looking back at her in the shimmering surface showed every inch of her nerves. She fussed with her hair, pulling one long curl over her eye in a way that could be interpreted as either seductive or careless. She flipped it back, but now her forehead looked too long. She brought a different piece forward, but it hung too low, catching in her lip gloss and sticking uncomfortably.

"Where can I find a couple of wineglasses?"

The words were muffled through the wall, and she yelled back a little too quickly and much too loudly, "I'm getting them! Be right there!"

Alison looked back at the mirror and took a deep breath. She tried one more curl and finally found the right look. Casually seductive. She smiled at herself and realized with a jolt that she looked slightly crazy. She tried a softer smile. Better. She lowered her eyelashes. Good. Stepping back from the sink, she smoothed the sweater over her stomach. She tugged at the waistband of her skirt. The elastic slipped a little lower on her hips. With one more deep breath, she turned and left the kitchen.

Jess leaned against the back of the couch, her eyes fixed on the bottle in her hands. She held her shoulders high and her legs stretched out in front of her. The pose was familiar. Nearly identical to the one she struck while waiting outside of Hibbs to ask Alison out on their first date. Alison had found her compelling to the point of irresistible that day, and she could not deny that Jess's power to captivate her had grown dramatically since. Her clothes hugged her curves in all the right places and exposed just enough skin. She looked like a Calvin Klein ad. Perfectly, elegantly at ease. Alison needed more than anything else to touch her and be touched by her. She needed it more than air.

Her knees were wobbly as she crossed the room and leaned against the wall directly opposite Jess, right next to the wide entryway to the bedroom at the back of her apartment. Beyond the door was her neatly made king-size bed. Alison forced herself not to look into the room. She slid her hands behind her, pressing her palms into the cool surface of the wall, her knuckles digging into the small of her back.

Jess looked up questioningly. "Glasses?"

She had completely forgotten to grab wineglasses. "I… um…They're all dirty."

"That's okay. We can pretend we're in college and drink out of juice glasses."

Alison smiled back, making sure the loose curl swung in front of her eye exactly the way it was supposed to.

"How about a corkscrew?"

Her nerves were so frayed, she didn't think she could move, much less walk. The idea of adding more alcohol to the mix was out of the question. She hesitated, biting her bottom lip. "I'm… not sure if I have one."

It was such a ridiculous thing to say, but she couldn't take it back now. Jess waited a long, agonizing moment before pushing herself up from the sofa and setting the bottle on the side table with an unnecessary amount of care. Her every movement was lithe, like a dancer. Alison didn't dare look away. Jess turned and the look in her eyes brought a flood of desire washing through Alison. Her gaze was alight. Crackling with intensity. She closed the gap between them agonizingly slowly. Alison held every muscle in her body perfectly still. The room was so quiet she could hear the rustle of her eyelashes when she blinked.

Jess slid close to her and stopped just before their bodies touched. She reached out with one hand and placed it, palm flat, against the wall by Alison's ear, then raised her other hand to Alison's waist. She looked down at her fingertips as they settled on Alison's hipbone with a touch light as a bird's wing.

She lifted her eyes until they captured Alison's. "Is this okay?"

Their faces were inches apart. Alison could feel the heat pouring off Jess's body and the breath of the words on her lips. Her voice failed her once again. All she could do was nod.

At that small show of permission Jess leaned in with her whole body, pressing Alison against the wall and capturing her mouth in a kiss so fierce it made her teeth ache. Alison's lips parted and Jess did not hesitate. She claimed Alison's mouth even as she pulled their bodies together. Alison's mind reeled and her body ached for more. More of her touch. More of her kisses. More of the solid weight of her body pressing her against the wall. More of everything that was Jess.

Cupping Jess's face in her hands, her back arched off the wall, bringing their hips together in a burst of desire. Jess groaned, pulling up Alison's leg, hooking her knee around her waist. She slid her hand under Alison's sweater. As her hands moved higher, she left a trail of sparks behind. Alison threaded her fingers through the strands of Jess's hair, pulling her face closer. Jess's fingertips reached the edge of her bra and teased along the lace-covered underwire. Alison could feel the corners of her mouth twitch up even as she deepened the kiss.

Her hand continued moving, cupping Alison's breast and thumbing the stiff peak of her nipple through the lace. Alison broke off their kiss and gasped at the touch. Jess moved with deceptive speed. She gripped the sweater with both hands, pulling it off over Alison's head. She leaned back in as the fabric drifted to the floor behind them, admiring the smooth skin she had uncovered. Her hand moved back to Alison's breast, palming it.

She teased, "Black lace? Were you planning on seducing me today, Dr. Reynolds?"

Alison wrapped her arms around Jess's neck. She traced the pad of her thumb across the dip at the base of Jess's skull. Jess shivered under her touch. "Maybe. That isn't a problem, is it, Dr. Baker?"

Jess's smile melted and she looked so hard into Alison's eyes that she felt as though her skin had been peeled away and she was wearing nothing but her soul.

"I've wanted you since the minute I laid eyes on you."

The breath was knocked from Alison's lungs and the whole world fell away, brick by brick, leaving just the two of them. Alison spread her legs, wrapping them around Jess's waist as she was pulled up into those powerful arms. She captured Jess's mouth, hurrying to take back what she wanted.

Jess broke the kiss only long enough to pant, "Bed?"

Jess carried Alison through the open doorway, her lips never once leaving Alison's. Jess's knees met the mattress a little too hard, and she only just managed not to tumble onto the bed. She lowered Alison down onto the comforter, and she pulled Jess's body down on top of her own.

Alison's fingers soon had Jess's shirt open. To her intense disappointment, there was a tank top under it. She growled, her fingers raking at the layer of cotton keeping their skin separate. Jess pushed herself to her knees with a chuckle and pulled the open shirt off her shoulders.

For the first time Alison was able to see the extent of the tattoos on Jess's arm. Bright swirls of color covered every inch of skin from her collarbone to her elbow in a dozen different shades of reds, greens and blues. The grace of the art was only marred by the strap of her black tank top, an issue quickly remedied when Jess grabbed a fistful of fabric and pulled it over her head.

All thought of art appreciation vanished from Alison's head. While Jess's breasts weren't overly small, she needed no bra and Alison was treated to a view of her naked torso. Her legs clenched reflexively, gripping Jess even tighter. Her eyes traveled down the plane of her stomach. It was flat if not defined, and Alison squirmed at the thought of the softness and swell of her own abdomen. There was another tattoo starting over one hipbone and disappearing behind the wide leather belt that held up her jeans.

While she had been studying Jess's form, Jess had been doing the same. Her hands began to caress the skin of Alison's stomach, and the sparks of desire that had lit before multiplied beyond measure. She gripped Jess's arms, trying to pull her back down but Jess pulled Alison up off the bed and unhooked her bra.

If she spent every future waking moment kissing this woman it would not be enough. The taste of her lips was mesmerizing. Like barely sweetened heavy cream. The feel of her lips. The soft brush of their tongues together. All of it together was paradise. A slice of heaven in a world that had been ordinary for far too long.

Jess moved her mouth to kiss down Alison's jaw and to her neck. Alison was finally able to pull Jess down on top of her, and their skin met in a thousand tiny jolts of electricity. She slid her arms around Jess's back as she extended the trail of kisses down Alison's collarbone to her shoulder.

The muscles of Jess's back were corded with tension. Alison raked her nails over them, feeling them ripple and contract. Jess's hips bucked forward seemingly of their own accord, and she raked her nails again, this time earning a groan. The cold metal of Jess's belt buckle pressed against Alison's bare stomach, and she ground her hips up against the denim-clad pelvis above her. If only she weren't still wearing her skirt so she could feel the coarse fabric against her naked skin.

Jess's lips found her breast. The heat of her mouth wrapped around Alison's nipple forced a whimper from her. As she teased with her tongue, Jess worked the rest of Alison's clothes off. It wasn't until she felt the chill of evening air that Alison realized she was naked. She wanted Jess's weight to settle on top of her, to hold her down and ground her in the moment, but Jess was moving again. Her mouth trailed down Alison's body, lips brushing lightly over her skin. Ribs, stomach, hips.

She closed her eyes, trying to prepare herself for what she knew was coming next, but it was a futile effort. The feel of

Jess's breath on the sensitive skin between her legs was intense, the feel of her mouth was enough to make her crumble.

Jess had barely begun when Alison's body started to shake. Her hands clawed at the comforter, twisting huge handfuls of goose down-filled fabric between white knuckles. She tried to hold on as long as she could, tried to prolong the time she could enjoy the exquisite touch of Jess's tongue where she ached for it to stay, but she was powerless. All she could do was close her eyes, bury her fingers in Jess's hair and hope that it would be enough to keep her anchored to the world around her when everything else flew apart.

Her body climbed to impossible heights and the crash of her pleasure came moments later. She shouted with her release and clung to Jess, trying desperately to hold her hips still while wave after wave of ecstasy rippled through her. All the anticipation that had built shattered and shimmered in the night air like the glittering glass of a car accident. A few tears leaked from the corners of her eyes as her body finally stilled. Realizing that she was gripping Jess's scalp with bruising force, she released her hold. She gasped for air, but could not find breath to speak.

Reversing the trail of kisses she had left before, Jess made her way back up Alison's body and settled in above her. Alison's body responded on its own even as she was still recovering. Her legs wrapped themselves around Jess's waist, pulling her close and finally reveling in the feel of denim against her overheated skin.

Holding Jess this close, Alison could feel the tension in her shoulders. There was a tautness to the kisses she pressed to Alison's neck. A rigidity of hard fought self-control. Alison reveled in the almost superhuman mastery Jess exerted over her own desire. She reveled even more in the chance to break it.

Slipping open her belt with their bodies united was a struggle, but an enjoyable one. They kissed hungrily while she worked, and, once she dealt with Jess's belt, the button and zipper quickly followed. In the space of a heartbeat, Alison plunged her hand into the space she created. Jess groaned and her hips fell into a quick rhythm to match Alison's touch. They rocked together, the speed and desperation of their movements increasing and soon she was forced to cede control to Jess, allowing her to set the pace. A few hurried breaths later, Jess shook herself apart. With a howl that sounded almost as much pain as pleasure, her muscles locked in the circle of Alison's arms.

She allowed Jess to almost catch her breath before starting to move her hand again. With another low moan, Jess's hips sluggishly moved to match her. This time Alison was slower, intent on prolonging their encounter. Jess, it seemed, wholly approved. Without interrupting the movement of their joined bodies, Jess moved a hand to Alison's thigh. The touch was gentle but insistent, and Alison obliged, opening herself wide.

Jess's touch was a powerful distraction, and for several long moments, her own movements wavered. Finding an equilibrium between her partner's pleasure and her own took some time, but soon enough they moved together, found themselves synched, and their bodies responded as much to their closeness as to their touch. They moaned together, sweat pooling in each spot where their bodies met. Alison ran a shaking hand through the dampening hair at the base of Jess's skull.

Jess buried her face in the pillow and screamed, her whole body quaking. The intensity of her release was enough to send Alison over the edge, and they held each other tight as they crested together. Their screams mingled and mixed, harmonizing in the same way their bodies had. Neither of them moved as their breathing slowed and returned to normal.

Alison's eyelids felt like they were made of lead when she registered Jess shift above her. She clutched at the shoulders she still held instinctively. "Don't go."

Alison's neck muffled Jess's voice as she shifted to lay next to her. She pulled Alison close, tucking her back close against her own chest and replying sleepily, "I'm not going anywhere."

Alison blinked heavily as she snuggled closer against Jess. She pulled her tattooed arm tight around her waist. When she blinked again, her eyes did not reopen.

CHAPTER TWENTY-FOUR

Alison awoke to the unfamiliar sensation of warm weight pressed against her back. It took several long moments of blinking away sleep before the memories came flooding back. A smile spread across her face. The feel of her nakedness under the stiff cotton sheets was almost as pleasant as the arm wrapped around her side. Jess's hand curled into a loose fist against her chest. She smiled and drifted back to sleep.

When she woke the second time, the windows glowed with pale, early morning sunlight. She lay on her back. Sometime in the night she had kicked the covers off and the chill of the air made her shiver. A hand splayed across her abdomen clenched briefly at the movement. Jess lay on her stomach, her face turned out from the pillow just enough so she could breathe. Her hand was low on Alison's stomach. Low enough to set off a series of pleasant reactions in Alison's body. She grinned as she looked at the woman beside her.

It was rare that Alison shared her bed with anyone. She'd found that the older she got, the less interest she had in sex with strangers. She hadn't always felt this way. She had, as Beth put it, kissed a lot of frogs in her youth. Those days were long gone. Now she actually had to like a person before she slept with them, so she rarely brought people home, and never this early in a relationship. She watched Jess sleep and marveled at how quickly she had fallen this time. But there was no doubt now. She was lost.

Jess's bangs, which normally stuck straight up in well-defined spikes, had been mussed about while she slept. Whatever hair product she used was completely gone. Alison couldn't help herself. She reached out to touch. The hair was soft and silky as she ran her fingers through it. Jess twitched and then blinked, her eyes peeling apart with difficulty. She struggled to focus first on Alison's face, and then trailed down the length of her body with obvious appreciation. "Like what you see?" Alison asked in a teasing tone.

"Yes, as a matter of fact." Her voice was thick and gravelly with sleep, and the sound had an even more profound effect on Alison than the hand on her abdomen. "I very much do."

She reached out and drew Jess over to her and into a kiss. Her eyes flitted back to the rumpled hair and she said, "So do I."

Jess tried to look up at her own hair and groaned. "It's terrible, isn't it?"

"No! It looks great."

"Liar. I can feel how bad it looks."

"It's a little…fluffy."

Jess rolled her eyes and buried her face into her pillow with a grunt.

"Aw, don't be like that! It's cute!"

The response was barely audible through the pillow. "You're making it worse."

"You look like a baby duck!"

Jess groaned again and rolled onto her back, throwing her hands over her face in a vain attempt to hide both her blush and the offending hair. The movement had the effect of exposing the majority of her body to Alison's greedy eyes. She must have discarded her jeans sometime in the night. Alison was able to look at her entire body for the first time. When Jess lifted her hands to her face, the muscles of her arms and abdomen rippled enticingly and the tattoo that dipped below her hipbone came into plain sight.

Alison's mind went blank. Before she had time to think, she straddled Jess's hips. Jess dropped her hands from her face, and the blush moved from her cheeks to her neck and chest. She slid her hands up and down Alison's thighs and gripped lightly at her waist. Alison canted her hips forward, increasing the pressure where their bodies met and earning an appreciative sigh from Jess.

She found she couldn't keep her eyes on Jess's face. It made her stomach flip and her eyes water. It was like staring at the sun. She traced the outline of the tattoo on Jess's bony hip with her fingertips and delighted in the way the skin jumped at the ticklish touch. The piece was a snake made up of blocks of different shades of green and teal pieced together to make a whole. Like a mosaic or a stained glass window. The tail brushed the extreme edge of her thigh, the body looping up high on her right side and circling above the point of her hipbone. The snake then swooped down again to just above the patch of hair at her pelvis before traveling back up and ending in a simplistic rendering of a face just below her belly button. Its two bulbous eyes were a vivid green the exact shade of Jess's.

"It's beautiful," Alison said, hypnotized by the curving lines and the shocking eyes. "What is it?"

Jess tucked her hands behind her head on the pillow, fully aware of how the movement accentuated her small, firm breasts and the muscles of her arms.

"A snake."

Alison gave an exaggerated roll of her eyes and shifted her weight off Jess's lap. Jess's hands were back on her hips in a flash, holding her in place. Alison hadn't the slightest intention of giving up her spot, but it pleased her to know that Jess wanted her to stay.

"Okay! Okay! You win. It's a Celtic serpent." Alison settled back into place and Jess left her hands on her hips as she continued, "I saw it on a trip to Dublin right after I got into med school. It symbolizes fertility and immortality. I got it done a couple of years later, when I decided to focus on obstetrics."

Alison's fingertips were at the face of the snake, where it was pointing to her navel. "Appropriate placement. Since it's about fertility."

Alison slid her hand down the snake's body as it dipped toward Jess's pelvis. Instead of following the tattoo's path toward her hip, she let her fingers continue their path down, through the patch of hair and between their bodies where heat was rapidly building. Jess groaned and threw her head back into the pillow, her hips bucking up into Alison's touch.

Her touch was teasing at first. She moved more slowly than last night, intent on exploring and discovering her new lover's body. Jess responded to each movement of her hand with the most wonderful noises. Her eyes closed tight, lines of strain already appearing on her face.

Alison slid her knees back along the mattress and Jess immediately spread her legs wide. Alison dropped to her elbows. She traced the line of the snake tattoo again, this time with her tongue. The wet trail her tongue left shimmered in the early morning light from the window, giving the pictogram the illusion of life as it wound around her hip. Jess's breathing picked up, and her hands, which had fallen nearly lifeless from Alison's hips when she moved, writhed on the mattress.

When she reached the tattooed face of the snake, she started back down, this time leaving a trail of light kisses. She abandoned the line of inked skin and moved her lips down lower to meet her hand. She replaced her fingers with her tongue, sliding her fingers further down.

"Ali! Oh God Ali!"

Jess spoke her name so quietly. It was a whisper. A prayer. Her hands fisted in the sheets. Alison moved almost hypnotically. She used each whimper from Jess's lips or shift of her hips to adjust her movements. She wanted to explore slowly, to enjoy every taste and every touch, but the pressure building in her own body was demanding attention and Jess was fairly shivering with tension beneath her.

Jess's body froze and silence swelled for a long heartbeat before she fell apart. Her back lifted off the bed and she was shouting what sounded like Alison's name, but the sounds were too incoherent. Her abdomen strained to hold her off the mattress. She fell silent again for a moment before flopping back down to the pillows. Alison slowed, but did not stop. Soon Jess was groaning again, and Alison picked up her pace. Her second release came much more quietly, her body locking and her mouth opening, but no sound escaped her.

Alison watched the display in silent awe. The curve of Jess's body and the smell of her skin was intoxicating. Finally, Jess slumped back against the bed and went limp with exhaustion. She kissed her way back up Jess's body, passing the tattoo and moving on up along her stomach and her heaving chest. She found Jess's lips and they fell into a deep kiss, their tongues lashing almost desperately against each other.

An arm wrapped around Alison and she was on her back. The kiss continued as Jess slipped a thigh between her legs, nudging them apart with an impatience only barely surpassed by Alison's. She pressed her hips up into Jess's thigh, craving friction to relieve the throbbing between her legs. Jess allowed her free rein, holding her close and kissing her expertly while she took her own pleasure.

Alison was going to stop, had intended to only go so far and let Jess finish the job, but her release was too close to be held back. She gripped hard at Jess's shoulders and buried her face in the crook of her neck as she screamed and fell over the edge. She tried to say something, anything, but she did not have the breath for words as wave after wave of pleasure coursed through her. Jess held her through it all, keeping her close until the last shudder rippled away and calmed.

She turned her face to Jess and saw an expression she couldn't read in those eyes so startlingly green. They were blank, but somehow pulsing with emotion at the same time. She looked into them for a long moment, trying to decide what she saw. Jess covered her lips in a kiss. Alison's eyes fluttered shut. Jess's lips were tender and eager. The kiss was not searching or insistent, and somehow it spoke volumes, translating the unreadable look from a second earlier.

If Alison dared name it she would have called it love, but she did not dare. Instead, she allowed her body to melt into the one above her and hoped, though she knew she shouldn't, that the kiss was saying all the things she wanted to hear.

CHAPTER TWENTY-FIVE

Bright, white sunshine pricked at Alison's eyes and threw straight, sharply defined shadows on the floor. She blinked and squinted from the deluge of light, turning over with a groan. She turned full into the smiling teeth of Jess.

"Hi there."

Her voice was strong and sure, without the faintest hint of sleep but instead an undercurrent of the teasing laughter that Alison remembered from their first meeting. She smiled back, her stomach flipping pleasantly.

"Hi."

Jess reached out and cupped her face, pulling her into a kiss. At every spot where their bodies touched little fires erupted under Alison's skin. She thought about laying back, seeing if she could pull Jess on top of her, but decided to wait.

Jess broke the kiss and lay back, her left arm draped casually across the sheet that covered her. The bright white fabric provided a stark contrast to the splashes of color on her skin. Alison caught herself staring. The tattoo looked like a swirl of many colors from farther away, so many images bundled on top of each other and sweeping together. This close, however, she could make out individual pictures.

There was a sailboat rocked by blue-green water. Fish whose scales somehow seemed to sparkle leapt all around it. On the boat was a tiny figure holding a fishing pole, the line laden with an unseen catch bending the pole almost to the point of snapping. Alison touched her fingers to one of the fish, half-expecting it to flop around and jump away from her hand.

"You like to fish?"

"Nah. Never did. I couldn't sit still long enough." Jess pointed to the tiny figure fighting to reel in his prize. "My dad loves it. He has a little boat moored at Hayden's Island. That's a little strip of land between Portland and Washington state. He spends every minute he can on it. Mom says she's lost her husband to the Columbia River, but it makes him happy, so she deals. He's a lot to handle, my dad. She probably enjoys the alone time more than she admits."

"A lot to handle?"

"He's got a lot of personality. Never met a stranger. Mom's a little quieter. She'd rather spend her day in the garden."

She pointed to another spot on her arm. A spray of sunflowers and some red-orange flower Alison couldn't identify. There was a butterfly among them and a jewel-bright hummingbird in shimmering green and red.

"There are hummingbird feeders all over the backyard. She'll kneel there in the dirt with this big, floppy straw hat down low on her forehead and watch the birds just zip between the blooms and the feeders."

There was a far-off, misty look in Jess's eyes. Alison watched her stare at the ceiling and smile, suddenly realizing it was more than the West Coast scene that she had left behind in Oregon.

"Are they still there? In Portland?"

"Yeah. They sold the place I grew up in to a pair of new arrivals with more money than sense right when the market topped out. Made a killing. So they bought a place in Vancouver, Washington. It's right across the river from the city. So I can… could go see them all the time."

There was no bitterness in Jess's voice, even at the reminder that she had moved away. She seemed lighter, happier than Alison had seen her in a while. The lines of exhaustion that sometimes marked her face were gone. She absentmindedly rubbed Alison's thigh through the sheet in a way that felt like contentment.

Alison lay her head down on the pillow, putting their faces inches apart. "They're beautiful. Your tattoos. Are they all by the same artist?"

"Yep."

"You must have spent a fortune on them."

"Not as much as you'd think." She pulled Alison's arm on top of her, dragging her closer so their bodies touched in a thousand more tiny explosions. "The artist I found was crazy talented. I waited ages to see her the first time. We got to talking while she was working and we went out for coffee after. We started dating. That got me the 'sleeping with the artist' discount. Barely paid anything for most of the half sleeve."

"Good deal."

"Yeah. About half of the women in Portland thought so too, so they got on board. Not even sure how she could afford to eat. I don't think anyone paid full price for her work. We were living together, but I had just started at Legacy and I worked long hours. Plenty of time for her to bring lots of people home. I was the only chump who fell in love with her though."

"Oh, Jess. I'm sorry."

"It's okay. Three years and three thousand miles is a lot of distance. It puts things in perspective. Besides…" She pulled Alison into a kiss. "I've got other, way more pleasant things to focus on at the moment."

There was still no hint of pain on Jess's face, so Alison pushed a little farther. "That's what you meant. When I brought up cheating at Babe's and you said it hurt the same if it was cheating with a woman."

"I have firsthand experience." She looked over at Alison. "So now it's your turn."

"My turn for what?"

"To explain what you meant that night. Why are you so sure that lesbians think you'll cheat on them with a man? I got the impression that was firsthand experience too."

Alison groaned and rolled over, suddenly feeling less interested in physical contact. "You could say that."

"If you don't want to talk about it I understand."

"No." She put a hand over her face to shield her eyes from the sun. At least, that's how she hoped it came across. "No, I can talk about it. Her name was Andrea and we were together for four years."

"That's a long time."

"Yeah. It was. A very long time. I met her at Babe's right after I got back to town from England. I had my first real job and she was...I don't know. I thought she was perfect. I sort of ignored all the little things she said at first about how bi girls are all sluts and stuff like that. I realized I hadn't told her I was bi. I don't exactly lead with that."

"You did with me."

"Yeah, well, I learned my lesson the hard way." Alison could feel herself turning inward. She didn't want to keep telling the story, but she had to finish it now that she had started. "It all kind of came to a head one night. We were living together by then and she said something to her friends that really pissed me off. I don't remember what it was now. She said a lot of things. I waited until everyone left and called her out on it. I told her I was bi and she just flipped out. We had a huge fight. I don't know how it happened, but I ended up apologizing to her for lying to her all the time we'd been together, even though I knew I hadn't exactly done that. She had a very strong personality."

Jess's hand slid onto her hip and she didn't want to hurt her feelings by moving away from her touch.

"Anyway, that's how it started. Then it turned into a little comment here, another one there. How she knew I was checking out guys all the time. How I was going to leave her and pretend like our relationship had never happened. And always about how I was going to cheat on her. Soon it was a daily thing. Breakfast, lunch, dinner, accusation. I spent half my day telling her how I would never do any of that, but the more I denied it the more it seemed to solidify with her. Then our friends would start saying things. I would catch the looks they gave me, and how they'd treat her like a victim. I should have realized earlier what she was doing. That she was spending a lot of time turning them against me."

"That sounds like textbook manipulation."

"One day I came home and they were all there, waiting for me. Our friends lined up in a big group on the couch, looking angry, with Andrea in the middle. They started in on me the minute I walked through the door. Someone had to stand up for Andrea, they said. To protect her from me. One of them had seen me on campus, talking to one of my students. A guy. They accused me of sleeping with him and they watched me while I packed some clothes and got out. I couldn't stop crying, and Andrea just sat there completely silent. A couple days later, I let myself in to try and talk to her. Try to get her back."

"Let me guess…"

"Yep. She was fucking one of our friends. Anna. They'd been hooking up for a while. At least a few months. Andrea called it a 'preemptive strike.' She knew I was going to cheat on her one day, so she beat me to it. That was my fault too."

"You know that's a load of shit, right? She was manipulative and terrible to you. Spending four years making you hate yourself? *She's* the bad guy."

Alison grabbed her hand and squeezed, a thin smile on her lips. "I have spent way too much time and way too much money on therapists who all told me that same thing."

"How long did it take before you believed it?"

"I'll let you know."

"Ali…"

She pulled Jess's hand up to her lips and kissed her knuckles, willing herself out of that place and back into this one. "The thing that was hardest about all of it was that all of our friends turned out to be her friends. They all backed her. Even when they found out about her and Anna. Even when she cheated on Anna with Emily. And on Emily with someone else. But I was the one they all believed was the bad guy, even after all of that. I was the one who lost everything."

"Sounds like you had awful friends."

"Except one." She let go of Jess's hand and smiled up into her eyes. A real smile this time. "Beth was there to catch me. And she waited almost a whole month to start with the 'I told you so's.'"

"I could have used a friend like that." Jess laughed. "Sounds like we have matching baggage. Lucky us."

Alison reached up and kissed Jess on the point of her chin. "Lucky me, anyway."

Jess threw the sheet over her. It fell over her eyes and she giggled as she struggled to get it off her face. The bed springs beneath her sagged then released. She fought her way free of the sheets to see Jess walking across the room toward the arched door to the bathroom. The sound of the shower spray hitting the tile wall drifted into the bedroom.

Showering meant getting out of bed. And getting out of bed always led to leaving. The last thing she wanted was Jess to leave. She frowned. She shouldn't have told the story. It had soured the mood and now Jess was going to make a quick exit.

Alison was working on a nonchalant script for when Jess got back from the shower and got dressed. Something that would encourage a call the next day without sounding pathetic if it didn't happen. Maybe she could even get Jess to stop by tomorrow night. Just a quick visit. Or a long one.

She groaned. What she really wanted was for Jess to come back to bed and stay there *until* tomorrow night. She should have just made a move when she first woke up. Why did she have to waste the chance with talking?

Jess's head poked around the frame of the bathroom door. "Are you coming or what?"

CHAPTER TWENTY-SIX

Lips pressed against the back of her neck. They were soft and smooth with just the barest hint of moisture. She thought the feeling was part of her dream until it came a second time, this time a little lower on her neck. The third kiss was almost between her shoulder blades, and her skin began to tingle. Alison whimpered, but the tiny sound was lost in the feathery mass of her pillow. The next kiss was directly between her shoulders and came with a whisper of fingertips on her back.

"Ali."

She whimpered again, this time loud enough for the sound to travel through the room. There was a soft chuckle behind her, and the breath on her bare back brought a patch of goose pimples to her skin. The lips moved lower, along her spine to the middle of her back, and the fingers grazed along her side. She turned her body, inviting the hand to cup her breast, but it moved away.

"Open your eyes, Ali."

She kept rolling over, falling onto her back. "Make me."

Alison kept her eyes firmly closed. She wasn't tired, she was blissfully comfortable. She had no idea how long she'd been in bed. It was just after noon the last time she bothered to glance at a clock. When she and Jess had collapsed, spent and exhausted, into bed still wet from their shower. There had been very little washing involved, and the water ran cold long before they finished. The light trying to force its way through her eyelids now was only slightly less intense than it had been then.

Warm, wet lips found her breast and held. Alison gasped and arched her back into Jess's mouth. Her body responded instantly. Despite the many times Jess had satisfied her since they returned from Charlottesville, she wanted more. Jess's tongue flicked over the sensitive flesh in her mouth and Alison's eyes fluttered open. Need throbbed painfully inside her even as Jess slowly withdrew her lips. She reached out to pull Jess back to her, and let out a frustrated cry when her hands touched fabric rather than skin.

Alison saw Jess's half smile. "You told me to make you open your eyes."

Jess sat up on the bed, fully dressed, down to her shoes, and her hair was damp. She had obviously tried to style it, but it was already falling at the edges as it dried.

"Hope you don't mind. I borrowed your toothbrush."

Alison stuck out her bottom lip and crossed her arms. Jess laughed and leaned forward, dropping a light kiss on her pouting lip. Alison held her in place, bringing her into a much less chaste kiss. Jess's shoulders relaxed and her hand moved back up Alison's bare side. She brought her hand to Jess's shirt, managing to free a button before Jess realized what she was doing and pulled away.

"Whoa! None of that. I have to get home."

Her words might have been a denial, but her eyes wandered back to Alison's naked torso. Alison slipped her hand under Jess's tank top. Jess tried to move away, but Alison was faster and her hand found its goal before she could dodge.

The rock-hard bud of her nipple pressed into Alison's palm, who smirked in triumph. "Still going to pretend you want to go home?"

Jess's voice was strained, but she removed Alison's hand from under her shirt. "I didn't say I *want* to go home. I said I *have* to go home. You know what I want, but I have to work tomorrow. If I stay here neither of us is going to get any sleep."

Alison's hand dropped to the wide buckle of Jess's belt. She sat up and eased the end free of the frame. She leaned in and kissed Jess on the neck, right at the base of her throat. When she heard the sharp intake of breath, she started to work the leather away from the hasp of her belt. "I don't need sleep." She kissed higher up Jess's neck. "I need you." She kissed just below her ear. "I need your skin." She had the prong out from the leather strap. "I need your hands." She whipped the belt out of the buckle entirely and went to work on the button of her jeans. "I need your mouth." Her lips rested right against the shell of Jess's ear, and she whispered, "I need your..."

Jess shot away from her as if she'd been electrocuted. Her shoulder banged into the dresser and a spindly-legged wooden giraffe figurine toppled over. Jess righted it, then fumbled with her belt, trying several times to re-buckle it and failing. She stopped, took a breath, and then managed to work the simple parts together again. She smoothed down her shirt.

"And that's exactly what I mean." She was grinning a little sheepishly. "You cannot be controlled."

Alison lay back on the bed, stretching the length of her body in one slow, fluid movement. "I don't remember hearing any complaints."

Jess watched for a moment, and then shook herself. "Thank you for proving my point."

"Fine. I'll let you go, but only because I want you rested when you take Beth to the operating room. When can I see you again? Tomorrow?"

"Not...um...not tomorrow."

"Tuesday?"

Jess flicked her eyes to the glowing red numbers of the clock on the bedside table. "Tuesday...Yeah. Yeah, I'm free Tuesday. Dinner?"

"We can start there."

"Okay." She moved toward the end of the bed, heading for the door. She stopped suddenly and turned. Leaning down, she kissed Alison hard. Hard enough to make Alison's head spin. She broke the kiss just as abruptly and walked to the door, dodging Alison's reaching hands.

"Bye!" Alison called from the bed, and received a wave in reply before Jess disappeared into the darkening living room.

The front door closed with a loud click. Alison rolled over and buried her wide smile in the pillow that still smelled like Jess. She took long, deep breaths and let the smell envelop her. Her mind drifted back over the last day and a half, and her body temperature rose with each remembered sensation. Of denim on skin and the press of grout lines from shower tiles into her knees. She lost track of time, reveling in the emotions swirling through her.

Her back and neck were stiff and aching by the time she rolled back over to stare at the popcorn ceiling. She was skipping, actually skipping, when she finally made her way to the bathroom for a long overdue shower.

CHAPTER TWENTY-SEVEN

im going to have to cancel for tom night
Oh, that's okay. I did take up your whole weekend.
something came up
I'll be at my office late tonight.
You could bring coffee and we could pick up where we left
off last time...
busy tonight
Too much to hope for, I suppose.
When can I see you again?
not sure
i ll call
have to go
see you later

Alison's Monday had started so wonderfully. She replayed memories of the weekend like scenes from a favorite movie. Just single frames of a dashing smile. The sound of intimate laughter. A whispered endearment. Then she got a text while heading from her classroom to lunch and the short exchange felt so cold and foreign that her world tilted on its axis. She knew better than to try to glean any tone from texts, but she couldn't help feeling like she was being put off. Sometimes Jess ran a little hot and cold, sure, but this felt different. It felt wrong. There was a sense of finality in her words. Maybe Jess had gotten everything she wanted and was done with her?

Once the idea wormed its way into Alison's mind, she couldn't dislodge it. She stared at the churning mass of students around her in the dining center, picking at her plate with no appetite. Eventually the smell of food made her gag, and she bolted from the building for the sanctity of her office. But the tiny room was less than inviting. She stared at the spot on the edge of her desk where she had sat with Jess standing between her legs, kissing her breath away. A sour taste filled her mouth. She turned around and nearly sprinted for an empty classroom. Her next class wouldn't start for a half hour, and it was possibly the most torturous thirty minutes of her life.

She could no longer deny that she was falling in love. She had thought Jess felt the same, but her brusque dismissal seemed to indicate otherwise. Alison went back over all of their interactions. She wanted to find evidence of attachment, but it was their colder interactions that floated to the surface. She found countless times when Jess had seemed standoffish, dismissive and aloof. She had thought at the time it was her manner. She was playing it cool. Each time she'd brushed it off with the excuse of a bad day, or the joke about being bad with women. The very line that had won Alison over now seemed to be proof against her. She wasn't bad with women. Alison had ample proof of that.

Maybe instead she was just cold? Maybe the awkwardness was because she couldn't even pretend to be interested? Alison tried telling herself not to read too much into it, but the timing was so obvious. Hadn't she seen this before? Hadn't she lived it before? Why had she been so open with this woman she knew so little about? It had been less than an hour since the conversation, and already she was wavering between tears and rage.

Class started poorly and somehow managed to get worse.

"I'd like a show of hands. Who actually read this week's assignment?"

The students looked at each other, fear in their eyes. Every hand went up, but they were hesitant. Wary.

"That surprises me because none of you seem to grasp any of the concepts we're discussing."

As their hands melted back down to their desktops she paced the room, prowling like a lioness who'd scented blood.

"Mr. Kim seems to think that Catherine of Siena was little more than a nun who wrote a few letters. Do you all agree with that assessment?"

They squirmed in their seats, resolutely silent. No one would meet her eye, not even the feminist in the back. She ended class early and everyone bolted gratefully to the door. Jennifer was so upset with her behavior that she was the first out of the room, sparing Alison little more than a hard look that angered her even more.

Her anger fizzled with no one left to vent it on and melted quickly into remorse. She wasn't really angry anyway. It was frustration taking hold, and in the end it just left her despondent. She sighed at the empty classroom. This would be a terrible semester. Her students deserved better. She needed to get a handle on her emotional life and she needed to do it now.

Her cell phone lay inert on the desk, cold and silent under the flap of her briefcase. Texting was a bad idea. She would never be able to get a straight answer. Worse, she would have to read their previous conversation to start a new one. It would only make everything worse. She couldn't call. Jess said she was busy. Besides, it would make her look crazy and clingy. Email was a safer option. She had emailed Jess a couple of times to make plans and to give her directions to her apartment. She closed her eyes as her stomach squirmed again with thoughts of Saturday. She shook her head and opened a new email, typing as quickly as she could so that she wouldn't think too much.

Jess,

I know you're busy and probably won't have time to respond—or even read this maybe? It occurred to me that we are moving really fast, but we haven't really defined what we're doing. Are we in a relationship? Is this just two adults having fun? I really like spending time with you and I just want us to be on the same page. Next time we get a chance to see each other, let's talk okay?

Hope you're okay.

I miss you.

Alison

She scrolled back up and reread the message. "Sure, I can send this. If I want her to run away screaming from the psycho stalker!"

She shook her head and deleted the message, trying again.

Hey!

Bummer about how busy you are. Drop me a line when you have a free hour so we can hook up. Know what I mean? ;)

If you can't find the time, that's cool. It's been fun!

See you whenever!

Ali

"Who am I kidding? I can't do this."

She deleted the second message and pushed her phone away. Her head hit the desk with a quiet thunk and she whimpered. She couldn't stop thinking about Jess. Her hands, her face, the sound of her voice. It was making her insane. It was as if her brain was waiting for her eyes to close so it could start projecting images of them together on the back of her eyelids. She wrapped her arms around her head and seriously considered letting herself cry.

"You okay, miss?"

Her head shot up off the desk. A middle-aged man with a cart full of cleaning supplies stood in the doorway. His eyes shifted to the scattered desks and then back to her. He wanted to clean the room, but he was clearly ready to run for cover at the first sign of tears.

She stood and snatched her things off the desk, not bothering to stuff them into her briefcase, but clutching them haphazardly to her chest instead. She rushed for the door and he all but barrel-rolled out of her way.

"I'm fine! Thank you! Sorry!"

She bypassed her office and headed home with her arms loaded down and her cheeks burning.

When she woke up the next morning, she immediately reached for her phone.

No calls, no emails, no texts. The silence had continued. She took several deep breaths and tried not to feel like she'd been used. She checked her phone again. The blank screen forced her to her feet. She repeated the same series of events after her shower, checking her phone in case the pounding of water on tile obscured the sound of the ring. It hadn't. There was nothing. She checked again after she dressed. And after she choked down breakfast. And after walking to campus. And before her first class.

She notched a minor victory by leaving the phone in her office when she went to teach, but her mood refused to improve and the people around her again afforded her a wide berth. Jennifer started toward her with a look of angry determination, but she didn't wait for the reprimand she knew was coming. She rushed back to her office the moment her students filed out. Nothing. She sat perfectly still, staring at the cold, dead shell of her phone for the entire fifteen-minute break.

She checked it again during her lunch break. Still nothing. She had to lock her office for the rest of the day and she actually managed to have a pair of meaningful discussions in her last classes. Her nerves were still on a razor's edge, and she practically ran back to her office after seeing her students off. She thought she heard a muffled electronic beep from inside, but was fully aware it might be wishful thinking. She dropped her keys twice trying to unlock the door.

She had a missed call.

And a voice mail.

She was too excited to check the caller before dialing in to her messages. The voice that she heard wasn't Jess.

Stephen was crying so hard she could barely understand him.

CHAPTER TWENTY-EIGHT

The Miller & Rhodes building held a special place in Alison's heart. It had been, bar none, the best, coolest and most popular department store in the city when she was a kid. The polished brass and the immaculate displays dazzled her. At Christmastime, they had had the best Santa in town and a wonderfully cheesy animatronic Christmas tree that talked and danced. The tree's name was Bruce the Spruce and he was the best part of every Christmas for little Ali Reynolds. She would stand there while her parents shopped and watch Bruce sing his songs and do his dances and, for that moment at least, the world was a perfect and magical place.

Malls had grown in popularity as the nineties loomed, and suddenly an old-fashioned department store in the heart of the city was the last place people wanted to go. It shut its doors, unplugged Bruce, and Christmastime for Alison got that much dimmer. The shell of the building became a hulking corpse in another decaying urban mecca. Eventually the wonderland of her youth was converted to a block of pricey condos.

Jess lived in one of those condos.

Alison stood outside the building and wrestled to control herself. The bittersweet memories that this building held kept her rooted to the sidewalk despite the chill that had finally settled over her hometown. Rain fell in icy sheets, dripping loudly from the awning where she sheltered. The rainclouds made a dark night even darker and drove the cold bone deep. Alison didn't feel the cold and didn't see the dark. Her anger warmed her from within. She stormed into the lobby and jammed her finger so hard on the elevator call button that she hissed with pain. The trip was a blur. In no time at all, she found herself rapping hard on a metal door with an artfully tarnished plaque displaying Jess's apartment number.

The Jess who opened the door bore little resemblance to the woman Alison had spent so much time with. The change was startling, and it kept Alison silent. There were dark purple circles under Jess's eyes, and the green of her irises was dull, like laundry left carelessly out in the sun to fade. Her shoulders hung lower. Her body seemed to fill less space inside the doorframe than before. Her hair hung limp. She wore a wrinkled T-shirt. Her tattered jeans hung low on her hips.

Alison's teeth clenched hard at the sight of her. Jess's dull eyes scanned her face as she leaned against the door. Her voice was just as defeated as her posture. "So you know."

Anger flashed in her white-hot. "Yes, I do. No thanks to you."

Jess blinked slowly. She was quiet again for a long time, and the tension inside of Alison ratcheted up another few notches. Finally, she pushed the door wider open and stood back. "Why don't you come in so we can talk?"

Alison looked past her into the room. The space would have been bright and airy during the day. All white walls, polished hardwood floors in a honey-blond tone and small cutout windows covering the far wall from floor to ceiling. Now the windows were black as pitch; a few low lamps fought and failed to dispel the gloom. There was a tumbler on the counter of the open kitchen half-full of a rich, amber liquid. Next to it was a tall, square bottle three-quarters full of the same. The metal seal and cap had been peeled off and it sat, coiled like a snake, on the far edge of the counter. Past the kitchen a plush, blue couch looked so soft and inviting, even from behind, that Alison knew it could lure her in if she let it.

"I don't want to come in." She turned her gaze away from the interior and felt disgust when the weak smile melted from Jess's lips. "What I want is an explanation. I want to know why you couldn't bother to pick up the phone and tell me what was going on. I want to know why you let me sit at home, oblivious to my best friend's suffering for two whole fucking days."

Jess's hand dropped from the door and she stuffed it into her pocket. "I don't expect you to understand this, but there are rules..."

"Fuck the rules!"

"That's not the way I live my life." Jess's eyes hardened, tiny lines appearing at the corners. "I have an obligation to my patients."

"But you have no obligation to me?"

"Of course I do. You mean a lot to me, Alison, but I'm a doctor. My job is highly regulated. There are ethical standards I have to live up to no matter what happens. A whole set of rules that govern who I can give information to and who I can't."

"Stop trying to hide behind your bullshit excuses!"

"HIPAA is not an excuse. It's a law and, incidentally, it's one I believe in. I have to protect the privacy of my patients." Alison opened her mouth to shout, but Jess stood straighter and spoke more quickly. "I don't have the right to tell anyone the private health information I have access to, no matter how much I want to. It's not mine to hand out."

Alison crossed her arms. "You told me about her private health information the day we met!"

"Beth asked me to tell you. To explain her condition. You aren't in the medical community, you can't understand..."

"I can't understand? *I* can't understand? My best friend is lying in the hospital fighting for her life! Her baby is dead! Her husband is a wreck! They needed me! She needed me!"

Jess squinted at the door opposite her own, her brow furrowing. Her voice was calm when she answered, "That's not a decision I can make. That's a decision that Beth and Stephen needed to make."

The truth of the statement cut through her like a knife. She hadn't known because they hadn't told her. They had waited until long after the worst was over to tell Alison anything.

"They just lost their baby. They weren't in a place to make any decisions."

"I know. I agree with you, but that doesn't change the rules."

"Well, that's great. That's just perfect. You follow your stupid rules. Meanwhile, people I love are hurting. *But you don't care at all do you?*"

She shouted so loudly that her last words echoed down the narrow hall. The lines at the corners of Jess's eyes deepened but her voice was still flat as a calm sea. "You're upset, and I understand that. Whatever you may think of me right now, I care about both Beth and Stephen very much."

"Of course you do." Sarcasm dripped from her words. "It's just me that you don't give a shit about."

Alison couldn't look at Jess anymore. Couldn't let herself see the pain and exhaustion, but they were unmistakable in her voice. "If you can think that after what we've shared…"

She cut the words off so that she didn't have to hear them. "What we shared? Am I supposed to believe it means something to you that I let you fuck me?" Jess flinched at her words and Alison found a kind of savage pleasure in the reaction. "Because if I believed that, you would have proven me wrong over the last two days!"

"Alison, please…"

"You talked your way into my pants, and then you disappear. Fine. It's not like this is the first one-night stand I've ever had. Just don't try to act like it meant something now that I show up at your door. You played me. Congratulations. That's it. That's all."

"You're upset…I get it. Why…why don't we leave this before we both say things that we regret? It's been a long couple of…Why don't we talk later?"

"I don't want to talk to you later. I don't want to talk to you at all. I don't want to see you. I am done with you. I'm done with being dismissed by you and belittled by you and used by you. I'm done with being your amusement for the evening when your video games just aren't doin' it for you. Or your tattoo artist is busy. Or you're finished bleaching your hair. Or whatever childish, ridiculous thing you're into next. You're an arrogant, emotionless, self-righteous hipster and I am *done* with you."

For the first time, something akin to what Alison was feeling flashed into Jess's eyes. She took a step forward and balled both hands into fists at her side.

"And you're judgmental, selfish and cruel. From the moment we met, you have refused to think about anything but yourself. Your own problems. Your own baggage. Your best friend just lost her baby and she damn near bled out on my table twice! Her dreams of having another child are as close to finished as they ever have been. She held him. Did you know that? She held the body of her son. Do you have any idea what it's like to hold… But the only thing that touches you is how it affects you. Not Beth, not Stephen, not…anyone else. If you knew what I…"

Jess stopped and the blood drained from her face. She seemed to be looking through Alison for the briefest moment, as if she wasn't in that hallway anymore. It passed in the blink of an eye, and her eyes cleared.

"I think you should go."

Alison was already standing in front of the elevator when she heard the door slam behind her.

CHAPTER TWENTY-NINE

Beth was too weak and in too much pain to sob, but tears ran down her face in a constant stream. When Alison had come to see her the night before, she had still been working her way through the anesthesia. She hadn't woken up at all during the visit. Alison just sat with her while Stephen told her the details.

They'd been preparing for another transfusion on Monday morning when the ultrasound showed limited fetal movement. They pushed back the procedure, monitoring him closely. His heartbeat weakened as they listened, and Jess decided they needed to take the baby. He was twenty-eight weeks, and with a bit of luck and the best medical care available he could make it.

Then everything went wrong. There were complications as soon as they started the C-section. Beth hemorrhaged just as they were about to get him out. The surgery, which should have taken an hour, stretched to nearly five. She lost so much blood that they could barely get it inside her faster than it was coming out. There was a long, agonizing time when Stephen was sure he was going to lose them both. Telling the story, he went white as a sheet and had to sit with his head between his knees before he could finish. In the end, they were able to stop the bleeding and sew her up, but her fight was just starting.

Her vital signs started to show warnings within hours of the C-section and she was back in the operating room without ever waking from her first sedation. A hematoma formed in her uterus. It was an extremely dangerous development. Somewhere inside she was still bleeding. If they didn't operate again she could die within hours. The second time around they only just managed to avoid a hysterectomy.

The baby wasn't doing much better. His heart had been straining when he was still inside, fighting an all-out war with Beth's immune system. Even a hostile womb was better than none at all, however, and now that he was out, he was losing the battle. Beth finally woke up Tuesday afternoon to find out that he hadn't made it. Jess came to tell them herself. Their son had lived for twenty-six hours, clinging to life inside the plastic box of an incubator. He never opened his eyes. He never felt his parents' touch. He was brave, but he wasn't strong. By the time his parents got to hold him, he was already gone.

Beth couldn't afford much strength to mourn. She could barely keep up with the events of the last two days, and she couldn't keep her eyes open. Stephen was a mess. He'd awakened Monday morning with a bright future ahead. Less than two days later he lay crumpled in Alison's arms. His son gone and his wife still fighting for her life. Then he said the thing that set Alison off completely. He stepped away from her and wiped his nose with the back of his hand.

"You should go see Jess. She took everything pretty hard. She needs you right now."

His words hit her like a punch in the gut. She'd gone to see Jess, of course, but neither of them had been remotely comforted by the encounter. Almost a full day later, she still felt a bitter pride in the words she said. The tears streaming down her friend's face only barely took the edge off her lingering anger.

She looked at Beth and struggled to find the right words. "Is Stephen at home with Rachel?"

Beth nodded.

"Is she okay?"

"She doesn't know." Beth took a shuddering breath. "After the last time…We didn't want to tell her again that she was getting a baby brother or sister and then have to explain if something went wrong. She's only two. It was so hard for her to understand."

Alison gave her a weak smile. "Maybe next time."

Beth shook her head and her tears were a river of regret. "There won't be a next time."

"Sure there will." Alison scooted forward in her chair and cupped Beth's hand in both of hers. "I know you're upset and hurting now, but you'll heal. Don't let them convince you…"

"No one is trying to convince me, Ali. No one's saying anything. Not yet anyway." Beth looked out the window. "Jess said she wanted to make sure we could try again when the time came. That's why she wouldn't do the hysterectomy."

Alison squirmed at the sound of her name, but Beth didn't see the way her lip curled.

Beth was still looking out the window when she said, "I just can't do it again. I can't do that to him."

She spoke as quietly as she could. "Your baby didn't feel any pain, Bethie."

They cried together for a long time. So long that Beth's eyes puffed alarmingly. When she was finally under control she whispered, "I meant Stephen. I can't put him through that again. I can't hurt him again. Give him a son and then take him away."

"Stephen doesn't think that way."

"We talked about it. He said it's my call and I'm calling it. We have a beautiful, perfect daughter. She'll be enough for us."

The tears came a little faster, and Alison held her friend's hand, feeling more powerless than ever before in her life. After a long moment, Beth gave herself a little shake and set her jaw. She looked at Alison with a decent facsimile of a smile. "I still haven't heard about your date. Jess could barely look me in the eye Monday morning so it must have been good."

"I don't...want to talk about it."

Beth's brows knitted together. "Ali?"

Alison stared at their hands clasped together.

"Oh God, Ali, what did you do?"

The anger bubbled up in her again. Beth, of all people should understand. "What did *I* do? Oh nothing, just sat around like an idiot for two days not knowing that my best friend..." She caught herself and took a slow breath. "And she couldn't even let me know what was going on? Couldn't warn me that something was wrong?"

"I wasn't exactly in a position to witness it, but I don't think she had a lot of free time to call."

"She had time to text me and cancel our date."

Beth squeezed her hand sharply. "She didn't have a lot of free time to call because she only left my baby's bedside to save me. She was with him every second until he..." She swallowed hard, her lip quivering. "And she brought him down to us herself. In her own arms, Ali. That's not what doctors do. They smile sadly at you and stare over your shoulder while they give you the bad news. Then they move on to the next case. Not her. She..."

Alison felt the tears prickling her own eyes even as Beth's cheeks started to dry. "I don't doubt that she cares..."

Beth cut her off. "Doctors also don't get to tell their girl-friends when something goes wrong with their patients. There's a law, Ali, and I've sued doctors before because of it."

"Don't go on about that. She lectured to me all about it last night."

"Then you know that she couldn't..."

"She should have warned me!"

"She couldn't."

"She should have anyway."

Beth smiled, but there wasn't happiness behind it. "And if she had, what would you have done?"

"I would have been here for you. I *should* have been here for you."

"Ali." The way Beth said her name made her heart sink. It wasn't the teasing tone that meant she was going to poke fun at her. It wasn't the conspiratorial tone that meant she was going to share a secret. It wasn't even the miserable tone she had been using all day that meant she just needed her best friend there with her. It was colder. She felt like Beth was farther away from her than she had been when an ocean separated them. "Ali, I gave permission to share my medical information with certain people. She has to live with my decision no matter how awkward it makes her personal life."

She had to ask the question, even though she didn't want to hear the answer. "Did you tell her not to call me?"

"No, I didn't tell her. I didn't have to. I needed time, Ali. I needed time to grieve with my husband." She made a point of looking straight at Alison when she finished. "Alone."

Alison flushed, and Beth saw it. "It doesn't mean I don't need you. Nothing is real until I tell you, Ali. I just needed…"

"I get it." And she did. She tried to show it in her smile, but the pain showed too.

"Why don't you tell me what you did?"

So Alison told her. She didn't hold anything back. The fight had been so raw, so harsh that she wasn't surprised to discover she remembered every word. When she got to the end of her story, when she had to repeat the things that Jess had said about her, she tried to pretend that the words hadn't touched her. The sick feeling of bile in her gut was obvious, though, and Beth didn't miss it.

"Wow. That was pretty harsh."

"It was."

"Are you going to apologize?"

"*What?*"

"You heard me. Are you going to apologize?"

"I can't believe you are asking me that. Why would I apologize?"

"Because it's the best way to get her to apologize."

"I don't want her to apologize. I don't want anything from her."

"Girl, I have known you too long to believe that. Look me in the eye and tell me you didn't sleep with her."

"Okay, I did, but I don't want to again!"

"Liar. I bet it was the best sex of your life."

Alison let go of Beth's hand, crossing her arms as she sat back in her chair. "After everything from the last two days, I am so not thinking about her that way right now."

Beth shook her head and grabbed one of her dreadlocks, spinning it between her fingers. Beth was waiting for her to say more, but she didn't want to examine what her heart was feeling about anything right now. Everything was too new. A fresh bruise that hurt just to think about, much less touch. She floundered again, searching for anything to fill the void.

"The worst part is she lives in the Miller & Rhodes building. Did you know that? I used to love that place. Bruce the Spruce was there. Now when I think of it, it'll be her I think about."

Beth rolled her eyes. "You and that tree. You were always obsessed with that silly singing tree. Anyway, Bruce the Spruce was at Thalheimer's."

"No he wasn't. He was at Miller & Rhodes."

She switched to a new lock, wincing as she stretched too far. "Thalheimer's had Bruce. Miller & Rhodes had the Christmas Tea. Don't you remember? When we were nine years old our moms took us. We got all dolled up with our dresses and our white gloves and the doorman at Miller & Rhodes held the door open for us and told you that you had pretty hair."

Alison thought hard and a flash of the older man in the smart uniform and cap came to her. "I'd just gotten a spiral perm." Beth nodded with a smug expression. She said almost to herself, "I was sure I was right."

"Ali, you have been my best friend since before time and I love you. But sometimes you can be very stubborn. And a little selfish."

"How can you say that?"

"You break her heart after everything she did for me and how much she's into you, but all you can think about is your ruined childhood memory?"

"It's not about…"

"Did you know Stephen and I got into a huge fight right before we got married? He almost called it off."

"What? Why?"

"Because of you." She plowed on through the pain on Alison's face. "Because he thought you were in love with me."

"He thought…"

"He was right."

The silence in the room was deafeningly loud. Beth continued, "He is right. And I love you too. Not that way, sure, but we do love each other, and definitely more than friends do. Even more than best friends."

Alison had never really thought about it, but it occurred to her now that she should have. "Maybe so."

Beth's smile made her eyes water. "No maybes. I love you more than almost anyone else in my life. More than anyone but him in fact." She was about to go on, but stopped and changed tack. "If you ever tell my mother or my daughter I said that I will never speak to you again."

Alison allowed herself a little laugh, but knew with a clarity she had never felt that Beth was being perfectly serious. The occasion seemed to call for something. "Beth. I…"

"Shut up for a second, Alison." She crossed her hands in her lap and looked at her fingers. "That wasn't an easy conversation to have. He told me some things about myself that I didn't want to hear. Same on my side. We weren't kind. I wasn't kind. I thought he'd never have me again after that. He left and I sat there in the dark all night thinking that was the last time I would ever see him. He couldn't possibly love me after what we'd said. But he did. And I did. And the point of this rambling monologue is that moment. That conversation. That painful, awful, heartbreaking conversation is the reason that I love him more than you."

Beth's smile was far away again. The one she was always giving him that made Alison's heart ache.

"Maybe you just had that with Jess. I hope so. I hope you did because, Ali, she loves you. She probably hasn't told you, but she does. I've only seen the two of you together once and I know it. You can see it coming off her like a heat haze. She's thinking about you when you aren't there, and I know you're thinking about her when she's not there."

Alison couldn't look away. Even when her lungs burned because she was holding her breath and her eyes stung with tears, she just stared.

"Don't lose her, Ali. For me. Don't you dare lose her. I want you to know what it's like to love someone more than you love me. I want that so much I cannot begin to tell you."

She looked straight into her friend's eyes and all that love she had talked about was right there on the surface like it never had been before.

"I wanna dance at your wedding, Ali."

Alison stood up without a word and ran for the door.

CHAPTER THIRTY

Alison found herself standing in front of the nurses station with no idea what to say. Fortunately, the nurses weren't paying attention to her. There were three of them huddled together in a group off in one corner, talking to each other and oblivious to the world around them. Alison waited for them to acknowledge her, but none of them did. Impatience bubbled in her stomach, but there was a healthy dose of indecision there too. It seemed inappropriate to try fixing her relationship with Jess here and now, but she knew she couldn't leave it for another time. Already it seemed the moment was slipping through her fingers.

Still the nurses ignored her in favor of their conversation. She was about to speak up and demand their attention when the sound of Jess's name filtered through the talk.

A tall, middle-aged woman with a rather unfortunate Roman nose and mounds of bushy blond hair pulled into a tight ponytail said, "Dr. Baker's taking this one very hard. She looks like she hasn't slept in days."

A young nurse sat back casually in her desk chair responded, "I know! It doesn't make any sense. She left before me the last couple of days."

"No she didn't," the first nurse said. "She went up to Neonatal Intensive Care on Monday night. The nursing supervisor told me. She was there all night with the baby. They had to call her back here when mom hemorrhaged. Night shift says she almost did surgery at bedside when they couldn't get an OR ready fast enough."

"So when she was here Tuesday, she'd been here all night?"

"All night. Then worked the whole shift and stayed until after the little one went." She paused and kicked the toe of her shoe with the other heel. "Sad. I can't believe what that poor woman went through and then to lose the baby after only a day."

The third nurse was Nancy, and she stopped typing into the computer to say over her shoulder, "Were you here when they brought him down? I can't get that image out of my head. Tiny thing."

"Weighed less than two pounds, I heard."

They were all quiet for a long moment, lost in their own thoughts. Alison's stomach was like a lead weight.

"Dr. Baker's the one who asked the chaplain to talk to us after he'd met with the parents." Nancy's fingers hit the keys harder as she continued, "Dr. Emmett would never have done that. Wouldn't have occurred to him how we'd feel."

The tall nurse crossed her arms over her chest. "And she's down in the Blood Bank now. Said they were pretty shook up. Wanted to thank them. Who's ever heard of a doctor thanking the lab for something? Especially in person." She shook her head and her eyes finally fell on Alison. She stepped over to the counter with a warm smile. "I'm sorry! I didn't see you there. Can I help you with something?"

Alison swallowed hard, trying to digest everything she heard. "I need to speak to Jess."

The nurse gave her a searching look. "Dr. Baker isn't on the floor at the moment."

"I heard." She leaned forward, the countertop cold against her bare forearms. "Where is the Blood Bank?"

Nancy came over and practically elbowed the other nurse out of the way, her expression cold. "The Blood Bank is on the first floor, but it is not an area accessible to visitors. If you'd like to wait here for Dr. Baker to return…"

Before she could finish the sentence, Alison was gone. She walked purposefully to the stairwell at the end of the hall and slammed her way through the door. She had only the vaguest idea where she was going, but she would walk the entire first floor a hundred times if that's what it took. She could at least check with the information desk when she got to the lobby. She had to talk to Jess, and she didn't want to do it in front of those nurses.

She only made it down to the third-floor landing before the sound of a door banging loudly open startled her. She stopped and looked down over the railing. There was a flash of a white coat on the landing a couple of flights down. She heard a muffled choking sound, and something in the timbre of the voice was familiar.

She knew before Jess's face came into view between the thickly painted metal handrails that it would be her. She knew from the strangled noise that she was upset. What Alison hadn't expected was the knife in her chest when she saw tears streaming down Jess's face. Another sob threatened to escape, and Jess raised the back of a trembling hand to her lips to stifle it. She didn't look up, didn't see Alison. Instead, she looked around the landing and bolted through a door to her left. When it closed behind her Alison could see the sign that read 'Basement Access-No Exit.' She took the stairs two at a time in her rush to follow.

Behind the door was another landing, this one dimly lit with only a single flight of stairs descending from it. This was obviously an area of the hospital not meant for visitors. The stairs were stained metal, the paint on the walls chipped. A smell of dust and machinery was heavy in the too-warm air. At the base of the stairs stood a door with a shiny padlock the size of her fist. She didn't see Jess anywhere, but the sound of crying echoed a thousand times in the cramped space. She had stepped down onto the concrete floor before she noticed the nook underneath the stairs.

Jess squatted there underneath the stairs. Her arms lay across her bent knees, her face pressed hard against them. Her whole body shook with tears. Alison's mouth dropped open at the sight. This woman, the same one who lifted her up and carried her across her apartment like she weighed nothing at all just a couple of days ago, had been brought to her knees. It was overwhelming. A sick pulse in her gut reminded her that Jess had probably been feeling exactly this way last night. She should have held her. Should have been a shoulder for her to cry on.

An image so vivid it wiped everything else from her mind floated across her vision. In it she had stepped inside Jess's apartment the night before. Had accepted a drink from the square bottle and sat on the comfortable-looking couch. Had spoken quietly instead of shouted. Had felt Jess's tears soaking through the fabric of her shirt and dampening the skin of her shoulder. There were other tears there too. Her own falling like drops of crystal and rolling down a slope of cotton covering Jess's back. The kind of tears that actually made you feel better instead of exponentially worse.

The image faded and the thick paste of sadness and regret slid back into her stomach. All that kept her eyes dry now was fear. Fear of how badly she had broken everything. Watching Jess, she knew there was barely the glimmer of a chance she would ever be forgiven. She'd had the opportunity last night to be the better version of herself. She'd had a chance then to comfort Jess and take back in kind. To be what Jess needed her to be. Instead, the woman who meant so much to her was here hiding, huddled beneath a staircase in a dark basement, crying alone. Alison had no doubt she was part of the reason Jess had broken down.

The guilt flaring in her intensified her love. She could feel her heartbeat in her throat as she moved across the cold floor. It thudded in her ears and blocked out everything else. She knelt in front of Jess and reached out a trembling hand. She watched her own fingers shake and then make contact with the back of Jess's head.

Jess may have missed the sound of footsteps on the metal stairs, but she couldn't miss someone touching her. Her head shot up and her back pressed protectively against the painted cinderblock. Alison moved with her, slipping her hand from the back of her head to her cheek. Her thumb wiped away the tears and she stared into her red-rimmed green eyes.

For a moment that seemed to last an eternity, Jess's indecision was plain. She almost leaned into the touch. Almost accepted the comfort. Maybe even almost threw herself into Alison's arms. But the moment broke, and anger swept across her face.

Jess shot to her feet, shoving Alison's hand off her. Her words dripped with the venom Alison expected. "What the hell are you doing here?"

Alison stayed on her knees, her head bent and the ghost of Jess's skin still burning on her palm. "I was looking for you."

Her voice was colder than the concrete. "Well you found me. Now go away."

She stood and squared her shoulders, taking as long as possible until she had to look into Jess's eyes. She knew she would see anger and hurt there, and she wasn't wrong. "I want to talk."

Jess scrubbed the back of her hand across her face. "I think you've done quite enough talking. I'm done. I don't have anything more to say."

She tried to shoulder past, but Alison stepped in her path. "Jess please." Jess tried to move around the other way. Alison blocked her again. "Please let me apologize."

"No. I can't do this. Not here. Not now. Not at all."

Alison reached out, but Jess grabbed her by the wrist and spoke through clenched teeth. "Enough! I said stop!" The grip wasn't painful, but it was firm enough to make her hold still. "You can't just bat your eyelashes and say you're sorry, Alison. The things you said…"

"Were horrible." Alison stepped forward slowly, closing the gap between them. "They were judgmental and selfish and cruel. You didn't deserve that."

"No, I didn't."

Alison took another step. She could feel Jess's breath on her face, but her arm was bent at an uncomfortable angle where Jess was still holding her wrist. "I hurt you because I was hurting, and I…"

She dropped Alison's wrist and grabbed her shoulders, spinning her around and reversing their positions so that Alison's back pressed into the wall. She crowded into Alison's space, anger flashing in her eyes again. "You were hurting? *You* were hurting! Again, it's all about Ali. Your feelings always trump everyone else's don't they? Don't they, Alison?"

She pushed away and turned to leave, but Alison grabbed the lapels of her lab coat and pulled her back in close. "Not anymore."

She would no longer be denied, no longer let Jess hold her at arm's length. She pulled Jess into her and their mouths came crashing together. Initially, Jess allowed the kiss. Her lips responded almost of their own accord. A moment later, her whole body went rigid. It was like kissing a marble statue. Still, the need in Alison kept her pressed to those cold, unmoving lips for longer than she should have. Finally she pulled back, but she didn't let go of Jess's coat, sure that she'd try to leave again.

Jess's face was livid with anger. "What the fuck do you think you're doing?"

The only thought running through her head was the one she gave voice to. "I love you."

"Fuck you."

"I love you."

Jess leaned in, spit flying off her clenched teeth as she hissed. "You don't even know what love is. You have no idea."

"I love you."

"*Stop saying that!*"

Her shout echoed in the enclosed space, and stole the breath from Alison's lungs. She stood there, leaning aggressively toward Alison, panting with barely suppressed rage. "You know why I couldn't see you? Couldn't talk to you after everything went wrong? Because I knew you'd act *exactly* like you did. I knew if that little boy didn't make it, you would blame me. You would hate me."

Alison's nails dug deep into her palms, even through the fabric of Jess's coat and shirt. "I wouldn't have…"

"I've known for so long that he barely had a chance, but I fought and I pushed and I put him and Beth through so much just because I didn't want to lose you. You know what that makes me? It makes me a bad doctor. It makes me an asshole."

"You should have trusted me."

"I couldn't talk to you because I just wanted one more day. One more hour even, of you being mine before you broke my heart."

"I thought you didn't want me. We made love and it was the most amazing night of my life and then you rush out of the house and I don't hear from you. What was I supposed to think? Then you text and it's so cold and I was sure I'd never hear from you again. It hurt so bad."

"I was up all night with him, watching him fight for life. Beth started hemorrhaging and I almost lost her too. How do you think I felt?"

"When I finally heard from Stephen…The first thing that popped in my head was 'thank God, she still wants me. This is why she didn't call.'"

Jess looked into Alison's eyes and her face softened.

She tried to make her voice strong when she continued, "You know what that makes me? It makes me a bad friend. It makes me an asshole." She pulled Jess against her, pinning herself to the wall with her body. "I took it out on you. I hate myself almost as much as you hate me."

"I don't hate you."

Alison didn't believe it. The body pressed against hers was still rigid. Jess still held her hands at her sides. "Yes, you do. And you should."

Jess didn't answer, she just stood there like she was carved out of stone. Alison buried her face in her neck, trying to block out her fear with the smell of the woman she loved. Underneath the hospital smell that clung to her, she could just make out the faint lemony scent mixed with musk. Her stomach flipped with desire, and she couldn't stop herself. She leaned in and kissed Jess's neck, just beside her pulse point. She could feel the blood pumping through the vein against her lips. It felt so good that she did it again, this time a little higher, her nose brushing against Jess's jaw.

"What are you…" Her breath hitched when Alison ran the tip of her tongue along the column of her throat. "What are you doing?"

She ran her teeth over the hinge of Jess's jaw and pressed her body forward. "Showing you how sorry I am."

She wrapped her lips around Jess's earlobe and sucked lightly, earning a quiet groan. She dropped one fistful of shirt and grabbed Jess's breast, kneading it roughly. She could feel the fight in Jess's body, trying not to succumb to what Alison was doing, but it was a losing battle from the start.

Jess surged forward, pressing Alison hard against the wall. She shoved a knee between Alison's legs and used it to wedge them apart. Settling herself against Alison, she grabbed the hand that still gripped her lapel and held it against the wall. Then she forced Alison's chin up with the other and smothered her in a possessive kiss. She shoved her tongue past Alison's lips and claimed her mouth, kissing her with an almost feral intensity.

Alison kissed her back with everything she had. More than anything she had ever wanted in her life, she wanted Jess. She wanted her to know everything she felt. She forced a hand between their bodies and tugged at the button of her own pants. She heard the plastic of it clatter to the ground as her force ripped it free. She had to tug at the zipper several times before it opened.

Grabbing Jess's hand from her chin, she shoved it roughly down. Jess groaned into her mouth. Alison canted her hips forward, begging with her body for relief, but the wordless request wasn't enough. She broke the kiss reluctantly and looked into Jess's eyes. They were glazed with lust, and fresh desire burned through her.

"Please, Jess."

Her begging had a profound effect. Jess bared her teeth and then lurched forward, sinking a bite into the bunched muscle of her shoulder. At the same moment, she buried two fingers deep inside Alison in one swift, unforgiving stroke.

It was too fast and it was too hard and it was absolutely perfect. Alison cried out at the burn inside her, but tilted her hips up and out to take even more. Jess didn't wait for her, she started a torturous rhythm. All she could do was throw her arm around Jess's neck and hold on, riding through the waves of indescribable pleasure. This was not the woman who had been so gentle and hesitant with her all weekend, but it was the woman she needed right now. All she could hope was that it was the woman Jess needed to be.

Even as her own release was building, she adjusted her stance, bringing a thigh between Jess's legs and pulling her hips against her own. In time with the rhythm of her thrusts, she moved against Alison, moaning as need coursed through her. They moved with each other, locked together in that perfect way that had come so naturally for her with Jess, but she had never managed to find so easily with anyone else. Every touch, every breath giving to the other exactly what she needed.

Alison did not allow herself time to think. She focused on the pleasure both given and received, knowing that if she strayed from that, even for a moment, fear and doubt would take her over. For all the turmoil she felt when they were apart, being with Jess let her feel instead of think. Here, in this moment, with the press of her solid body and the taste of her skin on Alison's tongue, she was able to quiet her mind. Able to trust in her heart and the healing balm of Jess's touch.

Lost in the exquisite rhythm, Alison's pleasure built beyond her limits.

"Jess! God I'm going to…"

Her warning came too late. She shouted into the warm flesh of Jess's neck, and Jess was not far behind her. Her body shook against Alison and the explosion forced a bark from her. The sound continued long enough for Jess to run out of air, and it ended in a whimper.

As the pleasure subsided, Jess's whimper changed to a sob. She pulled Alison off the wall into the circle of her arms, hugging her almost painfully close and dissolving into tears. Alison wrapped her arms around Jess, stroking her sweat-soaked hair and whispering love in her ear. When it seemed Jess's knees would give way she eased her to the floor.

Jess pulled Alison into her lap. Her tears flowed freely, soaking into Alison's skin just as they had in that scene Alison had imagined of the previous night. She held Alison close as she cried. Alison cried too, but her tears were equal parts grief and relief.

They sat like that for a long time, on the dusty floor of the hospital basement wrapped in each other's arms. Jess avoided Alison's eyes. She pressed her face into Alison's shoulder until Alison pulled her chin up so they could look at each other.

Her cheeks were pink and she stammered when she said, "I…um…I didn't hurt you, did I?"

"No you didn't." Alison blushed a little herself. "I'm sorry I came at you like that. I got a little carried away."

"I'm not exactly complaining." Jess allowed herself something like a smile before continuing, "I should have let you talk instead of being a stubborn brat."

"I haven't exactly given you much reason to want to talk to me." She took a deep breath and looked at her lap. "Jess, I…"

"You don't have to apologize again. I heard you. Besides, it's my turn to say I'm sorry. I said some pretty terrible things to you."

"I deserved them."

"No you didn't."

"They're true." She swallowed hard, trying to force the shame she felt back inside. "You were right. I am judgmental and I am definitely selfish."

"That doesn't mean you deserved it."

"Maybe not, but I needed to hear it all the same."

"Well you were right about me too." She took Alison's hand in hers and rubbed the pad of her thumb across her palm. "I've been crazy about you since the minute we met. I would have found a way to get you to go out with me no matter what. Then it turns out you're the best friend of my hardest case. I've known for a while it would take a miracle to save that little boy, and I got it into my head that...that if I didn't save him you would hate me."

"It isn't your fault, Jess."

"It all got wrapped up together somehow. Saving him and being with you. It felt wrong to date you and know the chances were so slim. I didn't want to fall for you, but I couldn't stay away. I know sometimes I came off as...uninterested. I thought if I kept you at arm's length it wouldn't hurt so badly when I couldn't work a miracle and you broke it off."

"I don't blame you for not being able to save him."

"I just wanted to slay the dragon for you."

"Slay the..." Their lunch at Burger Bach. Alison's stomach dropped. "Jess, that wasn't a challenge. I was just...We were just talking. I don't actually expect an act of chivalry. Did you think all this time I needed you to work some miracle for me to love you?"

"I know. It's ridiculous." She looked up and there were tears in her eyes again. "I just...Is it so wrong that I want you to think I'm a superhero? I mean, you're perfect! You're gorgeous and brilliant and funny and passionate and so confident. I just wanted to live up to you."

"I'm not perfect. Not even close."

"To me you are."

Alison dropped her forehead against Jess's. "You're sweet, but absolutely nuts." After a moment, she said, hesitantly, "How about...how about instead of trying to be a superhero, you just try to be Jess?"

"I think I can give that a shot. If you try to be a little less perfect."

"I think I can do that, but listen, it's going to take a lot of work. I've been caught up in my own world for a long time. I didn't really see what that meant until Beth said some things. Are you sure you're up for it? Up for dealing with me?"

"Yeah, I think I am. I love you, Ali."

"I love you, Jess."

EPILOGUE

"Okay, I know this isn't easy. I need you to breathe. Just breathe through the pain, can you do that for me?"

"It hurts! Aaghh!"

Jess checked her watch. "You're doing great. Just remember your breathing."

The pain subsided and she fell back against the pillow, her breath coming in labored gasps and her eyes closed.

"Great job! You're a champ. The contractions are coming closer now, so we're almost through this."

In what felt like no time at all, the pain was back and it was excruciating. She screamed to gain even the slightest relief. She could hear her teeth grinding together as the wave passed again, leaving her breathless and panting. "Jess, I'm scared."

"I know, but there's nothing to be scared about. You're doing great. The baby is just fine. Your breathing is great. Your pulse is fast but that's perfectly normal at this stage. You're in good hands here. Just make sure you don't push quite yet. We need to make sure of the baby's positioning in relation to the birth canal and do a final measurement of…"

"Jess! I need you to be my wife right now, not my doctor."

She looked over at Alison for the first time and saw the fear in her eyes. It was so palpable her heart shuddered. She yanked the steering wheel hard to the right and pulled up to the curb, ignoring the horns blaring behind her as she threw the car into park. She took Alison's hands in both of hers and held them, one at a time, to her lips. She kissed each knuckle, watching the lines of worry around her wife's eyes lessen with each touch of her lips. When she kissed the last knuckle, she held Alison's hands close to her heart and looked up with a half smile.

There was a distinctly different tone to her voice when she said, "You're in good hands, Ali. I'm going to take care of you from this day to the last." Alison's shoulders relaxed. "I'll hold your hand when you're strong and hold you up when you're weak." She was quoting the vows she'd read to Ali on their wedding day, and the light sparkled in her eyes the same way it had then. "I will hold you when you cry and when you laugh, and I'll do my best to make sure there is more laughter than tears. You will always be the number one priority in my life. I'll give you space and time, but I'll never give you up. I'll be your biggest fan and your second best friend. I'll…"

Alison pushed herself awkwardly forward and pulled Jess into a heated kiss. If they hadn't been in a cramped SUV with people on the sidewalks all around them, she would have thrown the old pillow out from behind her back and dragged Jess on top of her, even with her swollen belly in the way. Instead, she held her wife close in a deep, promising kiss. It ended in a scream as another contraction rocked her.

Jess jumped back in surprise. "Hospital! Right! Hold on, baby." She looked down at the massive bump of her wife's belly. "You hold on, too, baby."

She gunned the engine and just caught the tail end of a green light, leaving twin S-shaped skid marks behind her. Alison's knuckles were white on the door handle, both from pain and fear of Jess's driving.

* * *

Jess paced back and forth endlessly. She counted her steps. Seven steps to the right brought her to the end of the hallway. She spun on her heel and took seven steps back until she reached the edge of the neighboring patient's door. Four more to the closed door to Alison's room. Check her watch. Spin on her heel and eleven steps back to the end of the hall. Spin, step, check watch, spin, step, spin, watch, spin, step, spin, angry muttering.

Every time she neared the stranger's door, the woman inside would shoot her a curious look. Jess ignored her and paced. Ignore, spin, step, spin, step, watch, ignore, spin, step. The woman's look became less curious and more annoyed. Spin, step, spin, step, watch, ignore, spin, step.

The sound of scurrying feet from down the hall broke her rhythm. She looked up just in time to see Stephen hurry around the corner, the tread of his tennis shoes squeaking on the waxed floor. A little girl with bushy pigtails was balanced on his hip. He was pulling Beth behind him, their linked hands stretched as far as they could go, Beth trying gamely to keep up in a power suit with a pencil skirt and four-inch heels.

Stephen looked like he might throw up at any moment: sweat stood out plainly on his brow and he was pale as a ghost. The panic in Beth's eyes made her look like a wounded deer. The only one of the trio who appeared to be having a good time was their daughter. She had a construction paper replica of a graduation cap perched between her pigtails and a certificate waving in her hand that read Kindergarten Graduate!

"Hey! Sorry!" Beth shouted down the hall the minute she saw Jess. "Sorry! We got held up."

"I graduated!"

The joy on the toddler's face was enough to smooth over Jess's irritation. "Congratulations, Little Bit!"

Beth grabbed Jess's hand with clammy palms. "Is she okay? What's wrong? Is everything okay? What happened?"

"Everything's fine."

"What's wrong with Auntie Ali?"

"Nothing's wrong, Little Bit. Remember what your mom and dad told you about Aunt Ali and the special doctor?"

She nodded importantly, her little paper cap bobbing. "Mommy and Daddy made a baby and put it in Auntie Ali's belly to get big and strong so I can have a little brother or a little sister. I really want a little brother though, so that's what Auntie Ali made." She grinned wide, showing several gaps between tiny Chiclet teeth. "She's a sherbet!"

Jess raised an eyebrow at Stephen, who adjusted the little girl higher on his hip. He shrugged and said, "Surrogate is a really hard word. Plus, she likes rainbow sherbet."

"Aunt Jess, can I have some rainbow sherbet?"

Beth patted her back. She wasn't really paying attention and patted a little too hard. "Not right now, sweetheart."

Rachel turned to stick out her bottom lip at her mother.

"That's right! She's been carrying your brother around for your parents while he grows up big enough to come out and meet you. Now he's all done." She turned her attention back to Beth and Stephen. "Are you ready to meet your son?"

Beth barely managed to capture a little sob before it escaped her throat. She nodded and grabbed her husband's arm. He didn't even try to hold back his tears, they slid down his cheeks and rolled off his chin onto Rachel's lavender dress.

Jess turned, but Beth grabbed her arm. "Wait!"

"What?"

Stephen looked at her. "What's wrong, babe?"

"Nothing." Beth swallowed. Her fingers bit into Jess's bicep. "What...what color is the wallpaper?"

"What?"

Beth shook her head and a single, fat tear fell from her eyes as she closed them. "In Ali's room. What color is the wallpaper?"

Stephen adjusted Rachel on his hip. "Beth, honey, we can just go inside and..."

"No! Just..." She looked back at Jess, whose heart broke at the yearning in her eyes. "Please tell me what color it is."

"Green." She put her hand over Beth's and the grip relaxed to something less painful. "It's not wallpaper. Just paint. Kind of a mint green I guess."

"Green."

Rachel started picking at one of the fabric flowers on the front of her dress.

Beth gave a watery smile. "Green. The rooms in Labor and Delivery are green."

She let go of Jess's arm, smoothing out the nonexistent wrinkles on her blazer. Jess waited another moment before asking, "Ready?"

Beth and Stephen both nodded.

Jess opened the door. She stood back and let the family go in ahead of her. Alison lay on the bed, a bundle in her arms with a tiny fist protruding from it. The others rushed in, but Jess stayed in the doorway, her eyes fixed on the glowing face of her wife. They had met in this very hospital, just one floor below where she lay now. Her face was puffy and she looked tired, but, as she handed her best friend the baby boy she hadn't been able to carry herself, Jess remembered the way she looked that day. The light in her eye was the same as it was now, but everything they had been through together, from a chance meeting at a bar to the day they said "I do," made the light shine all the brighter.

All the emotions that had been building in Jess since they arrived in the Labor and Delivery unit just a few short hours ago swelled impossibly high. They swept her up and carried her away. Alison turned and smiled at her, and the whole world stood still.

Bella Books, Inc.

Women. Books. Even Better Together.

P.O. Box 10543
Tallahassee, FL 32302

Phone: 800-729-4992
www.bellabooks.com